About the Author

Jerry lives in Salem, Oregon with his husband and son, and a very opinionated cat. He's had a life-long interest in all areas of the Titanic story. He also collects all things Titanic, as well as gramophones, recordings, and lives in a house crammed with books.

One April Night

Jerry Sacher

One April Night

Vanguard Press

VANGUARD PAPERBACK

© Copyright 2024
Jerry Sacher

The right of Jerry Sacher to be identified as author of
this work has been asserted by him in accordance with the
Copyright, Designs and Patents Act 1988.

All Rights Reserved

No reproduction, copy or transmission of this publication
may be made without written permission.
No paragraph of this publication may be reproduced,
copied or transmitted save with the written permission of the
publisher, or in accordance with the provisions
of the Copyright Act 1956 (as amended).

Any person who commits any unauthorised act in relation to
this publication may be liable to criminal
prosecution and civil claims for damages.

A CIP catalogue record for this title is
available from the British Library.

ISBN 978 1 80016 884 8

This is a work of fiction. Names, characters, businesses, places, events and
incidents are either the product of the author's imagination or used in a
fictitious manner. Any resemblance to actual persons, living or dead, or
actual events is purely coincidental.

*Vanguard Press is an imprint of
Pegasus Elliot Mackenzie Publishers Ltd.*
www.pegasuspublishers.com

First Published in 2024

**Vanguard Press
Sheraton House Castle Park
Cambridge England**

Printed & Bound in Great Britain

To Dean, Cylis, Rob, and Nicky.

Acknowledgements

I wish to thank everyone who has read, proof read and commented on *One April Night*, and especially all the members of the Titanic community for your advice and help.

Monday, April fifteen, 1912, two-eighteen a.m.

"Come on, jump and I'll follow you!" Andrew shouted above the rumbling noise from all around them. Matthew held onto Andrew's hand for a brief second, squeezing, as they gave each other silent encouragement. Then Matthew jumped.

Andrew watched him hit the water, which was now only a few feet below. He took a step off the edge of the deck and leaped. The water was bitterly cold, like a thousand knives being driven into his body. He could barely breathe, but he had to find Matthew. Andrew looked behind him as the lights blinked and went out and the ship towered above him in the darkness. People were jumping, splashing near him, crying out.

He thought he heard someone calling his name, so he swam toward the sound. He only got a few feet before he was showered with pieces of glass, wood, and scraps of metal and sparks; the screech of tortured steel drowned out all other noise, except the voice that persistently called his name.

An arm reached out and grabbed Andrew around the neck pulling him under, but he somehow managed to break free. He came up next to a collapsible boat with a handful of people huddled together inside watching the scene unfold in front of them. Andrew hung onto the side of the boat and followed their gaze.

The ship was breaking in half, sparks lighting up and rooms laid bare, the two remaining funnels toppling over. He barely missed being whipped by a torn cable. The forward half of the ship plunged under the surface, sucking in ocean, people, and wreckage along with it. He felt the water pulling him backward, but a pair of strong arms grabbed him and drew him aboard the boat. He sat on the bottom and lay against another man's body. Outlined in the darkness, he saw two men near him with boards, paddling the boat away from the ship. He looked from them back to the *Titanic*.

The stern was being pulled vertically, towering above them, and hanging there. The propellers lifted high above their heads, glistening in the dark. What remained of the ship started moving downward, slowly at first—and then the *Titanic* was gone.

"Where is Matthew?" Andrew fought off the stinging cold. He replayed the last time he had seen Matthew before they'd jumped overboard, and he wished he had told Matthew that he loved him.

After a while, the ocean became deathly silent; only a handful of the hundreds of people in the water had made it onboard Andrew's boat. It sat low in the sea because nobody had raised the canvas sides.

Andrew remembered the strong hands that had pulled him onboard; he could still feel the man's body against his own. He turned around to the figure who sat next to him in the dark and shook the man's shoulder.

"Thank you," he said in a rough voice that he barely recognized as his own.

He received no reply. The man sat upright, with his head bowed as if he were sleeping. He wasn't sleeping. But it wasn't Matthew. Andrew spent the rest of the long night staring into the dark, wondering what had happened to Matthew and William and so many others on a voyage that had begun just four, or was it five, days ago.

Andrew hugged his arms close to his body.

Chapter One

March twenty-nine, 1912 Edinburgh, Scotland

Andrew Elliot closed the book with a loud snap and put it back on the bookshelf. His mother called again from outside the library.

"Come on, Andrew. Everyone has gone into the drawing room, and your father is going to make the announcement."

"I'll be there shortly," Andrew replied. He paused, staring at the spine of the book, then turned to leave the room. Passing the weathered oak desk, Andrew saw the letter he had started writing earlier in the evening. He had not gotten past the opening greeting before he had to dress for dinner. He pulled out the chair to sit down and begin writing, but the door swung open, and his mother, Lady Alice Elliot, came in. He stood up once more.

"Everyone is waiting, dear. Are you coming to join us?"

"I'm sorry. I was looking for something, got distracted, and lost track of time," Andrew said in a monotone.

"You're sure that's all?" his mother asked, reaching out to take his hand.

"I'm fine. I would tell you if I wasn't." Andrew managed a smile. His mother didn't look convinced, but she kept silent.

Andrew came to her side, and she walked arm in arm with him out of the library, across the marbled floor, and into the drawing room. Andrew's grandmother and his uncle, Donald, were seated on a sofa by the fireplace. In small groups around the room were his three cousins, his father's two sisters and their husbands, and two of his friends from Oxford who were in town. In front of the gramophone, his father, Sir Macintosh Elliot, stood with Claire Bennett, a young woman with auburn hair, who was sliding the beads of a long pearl necklace between her fingers. Her brother William, a tall, rather pale young man with a moustache, stood next to them, alternately joining their conversation, and looking through the records on the table behind him. The three of them stopped their actions when they saw Andrew and his mother in the doorway.

Sir Elliot rang the side of his cup with a spoon, and the guests became silent. "Everyone, I invited you all here tonight to announce that my son, Andrew, and Miss Claire Bennett are going to be married," Sir Elliot said proudly.

The words sounded like a death sentence to Andrew, and he wanted to back out of the room.

His mother walked him across the room to join his father and the others, and Sir Elliot joined Andrew's hand with Claire Bennett's. There were gasps of delight and light applause, and one by one the invited company came to congratulate Andrew and Claire. Andrew stood by Claire's side, watching her blush and press people's hands; she clearly looked happy. He smiled mechanically, listening to only half of what Claire and his parents were saying. Andrew felt numb, his body only working as if a key had wound him up.

During dinner Andrew barely listened to the conversations that went on around him, and he only answered when nudged by Claire or prompted by his parents. He was glad when the dessert plates had been cleared and the ladies got up from the table to take coffee in the drawing room. He remained with his father, William, and the other men, listening to them talk about the coal miners' strike, an idea for minimum wage, and Scotland's win over Ireland in football a couple of days earlier for a score of four to one. When it was time to leave the room and join the women, William stopped Andrew at the door.

"I do hope this coal thing won't interfere with our plans to sail next month." William's hand lingered on Andrew's shoulder until Andrew moved away.

"I wouldn't worry, William. I'm certain everything will go as planned," Andrew said, trying to make his tone friendly, but it was edged with a mix of sarcasm and sadness, neither of which William seemed to catch. William smiled, shrugged, and walked away to catch up with Andrew's father.

Andrew hung back, wishing that Robert Craig was there with him, but Robert was only the son of the caretaker of the Elliot country estate and probably wouldn't be allowed in the drawing room, anyway.

Robert always seemed to know about what was going on in politics and sport, and Andrew could hear his voice teasing him.

"You spend too much time reading all those dusty books and writing, lad. There's a big world out there. I'll just have to get you out to see it."

None of that is going to happen now.

Andrew returned to the library after the last relative departed. As he sat over the unfinished letter, the door swung open, and his father came in.

"Claire and your mother have likely gone to bed, and William is going up shortly," Sir Elliot said. He took a cigar out of a box and lit it.

Andrew set the pen down again, put the note in a clasped notebook, and slid it into a drawer. He turned in his chair to face his father.

"You haven't once asked me how I feel about this engagement, Father."

"Because I expect you to be happy about it. It'll be the perfect cure for your ailment."

"I'm not sick, as you put it. I'm just curious how much you know about this girl, and I'm sure there are plenty of other eligible women in Edinburgh or London who would be a perfect match for your *wayward son*," Andrew said, gripping the arms of the chair.

Sir Elliot had come up from London shortly before the Christmas holiday with Claire and William, he had been introduced to them at a club dinner and was quite taken with Claire's charming smile and her good looks, shining auburn hair, and green eyes.

"That's not my business to know anything about her. That's your job. This voyage to America for three months will give you every opportunity to get to know her. Her brother, William, will chaperone. Meanwhile, your mother and I will prepare for the ceremony, and it will all be ready when you return." Sir Elliot avoided any mention of other available girls.

Andrew sighed. "Anything else you expect from me?"

"I expect you to marry this girl when you return, to be happy, to have Elliot grandchildren, and to forget all about this nonsense you were involved with in the country. That's the reason why you're going on this trip, boy, to prevent word from getting around outside the family, and prevent a scandal. A good ocean voyage is the perfect cure for anyone. Maybe you'll give up writing. That's an odd job for young men, anyway." Sir Elliot settled into a chair, looking up at his son.

"You think sending me on a trip across the ocean with Claire and her brother is going to 'cure' me of anything? Since their arrival here, we've been to every dance, museum, theater, and social function from here to London, and I don't know why, but I don't like her much. As for her brother, he seems like a josser to me."

Andrew followed his father's lead and moved to sit in front of the fire, which was dying in the grate.

"They come from a good family, a very long line of peers on one of the Channel Islands—Herm, I believe Claire told me. She and her brother were born and raised there," Sir Elliot said.

Andrew looked away toward the fire. "We're not living in medieval England anymore that you need to choose who I should marry. And who told you that she would be a good match?" Andrew inquired.

"When it's for your own good, and as long as you're under my roof, I can make any decision I choose," Sir Elliot said.

"The travel arrangements have been made, just like the engagement. Everything has been planned for me." Andrew tried to hide the bitterness in his voice.

"Yes, you sail April the tenth from Southampton to New York, and return in July in time for the wedding. But in the meantime, would you please stop walking around here like you've received a death sentence, and forget about your friend in the country. His father is making plans for him as well."

"What plans have been made for Robert?" Andrew asked.

"Nothing that should concern you, but you'll not be seeing him again anytime soon."

"Who won't we be seeing anytime soon?" Lady Elliot asked from the doorway. Both Andrew and his father looked in her direction, surprised to see her standing there. She entered and closed the door behind her.

"Nothing, Mother. Father and I were discussing some business," Andrew said. He didn't like lying to his mother, but the warning look in his father's eyes told him not to mention their conversation. His mother came in and sat on the arm of Andrew's chair.

"It's late, and everyone has gone up already. You both should do the same. We can talk about things tomorrow," she said with a smile, gently tugging at Andrew's hand, but he remained seated.

Sir Elliot got up and addressed his wife. "See if you can talk some sense into this boy. I give up. Good night." Sir Elliot left the library and closed the door behind him.

"This whole engagement seems so rushed. No wonder you're moody."

"I'm not out of sorts, Mother. Truly, it's just that I don't think Claire is the right person for me, and Father thinks he can fix me by getting me married off to someone that hardly anyone knows."

"Fix you? You're not broken that I can see."

"Then talk to Father and call this off, please," Andrew pleaded. "I would agree with you about Claire and her brother, William.

"For two people who claim to travel about so much, they only have one trunk between them, and I can't find any information about the family history in *Burke's*

Peerage. Strange, don't you think?" she observed, and Andrew nodded.

"Since they arrived here around the Christmas holidays, they've charmed everyone, but I think they're nothing more than fortune hunters. Surely Father can see that."

"I think there's something in what you say, but your father has made his decision, and you know what it's like to change his mind."

"Yes," Andrew said, recalling that his older brother, Thomas, had wanted to join the Army right out of Oxford, but his father had plans for him to go into government. It had been the cause of many bitter arguments and late-night discussions in the Elliot house. His father relented only when he discovered that an old school friend of his commanded a regiment in India and would take Thomas to serve under him.

Andrew's mother got up, but her hand lingered on his arm. "Well, Andrew, I'm going up now, and you should too."

"I want to write a letter, but I'll go to bed soon. Good night," Andrew said as his mother kissed him on the forehead and left the room. Andrew moved to the desk and sat down. He found his unfinished note in the drawer in the clasped notebook where he'd placed it. He took it out and dipped the tip of the pen into an inkwell. At the end of the opening sentence, he paused. He could hear the patter of rain outside the window, and he remembered another rainy day and a warm kiss. He closed his eyes tight and tried to relive that day with Robert, but the chiming of the mantel clock woke him up.

Andrew watched from the doorway as a footman loaded his luggage onto the rear of a carriage drawn by two horses that stamped impatiently on the pavement in front of the house. The driver steadied the animals as a motorcar rattled by and turned a corner. Behind him, he heard his parents' voices from the drawing room. He couldn't understand their conversation, but a few seconds later, his mother came out and joined him to watch as the last trunk was lifted onto the carriage and tied down.

"What's wrong, Mother? You're not still upset that I'm leaving, are you?" Andrew finally asked, breaking the silence between them.

She took his hand in her own. "I promised myself that I wouldn't spoil your journey, but…" She paused, looking over her shoulder to make sure she was alone with Andrew before she continued.

"You're sailing on the ship they say is unsinkable, and to make such a boast is flying in the face of God. It makes me uneasy, Andrew."

"I'll be fine, Mother, truly. I'll be in London with Uncle Max and Aunt Olivia until the tenth, and they'll make sure I get on the ship and see that it's safe," Andrew said, suppressing a chuckle. His mother was going to say something more, but Sir Elliot joined them.

He looked at the carriage loaded with luggage waiting in front of the house and then clapped his son on the shoulder as the footman walked toward them.

"The taxi is coming from the rank, sir, and will be here directly. The baggage will follow it to the station," the footman said, then went away.

They walked down the steps from the house toward the carriage to check on the luggage. Along the fence in front of the house, the servants gathered to see him off.

The three of them stood together for a moment or two, and in an attempt to lighten up the parting, Sir Elliot said, "I hope you're a better sailor than your mother. On the Channel boat, she lies in bed wrapped in blankets..."

"And your father always bursts into the room, letting in the cold air, and insists on pointing out how well the boat is handling the sea," she finished her husband's sentence, and it made Andrew smile to see the playful teasing between them.

"I'll be sure not to write about how the ship handles the ocean waves. What do you want me to bring you back from America? Indian beads or buffalo skins, or maybe a cowboy hat with an arrow through it?" Andrew said.

"We'll be satisfied with a boring postcard of some monument or other. *Wish you were here* scrawled on the back," his father said.

They looked at the footman coming toward them across the walk. Andrew felt his mother touch his arm.

"I hope those two come down soon, or you'll miss your train. Mac, go upstairs and see if they're ready," she said. His father grumbled and checked his pocket watch. Sighing, he went back into the house.

Andrew and his mother stood alone, watching the servants checking the luggage on the back of the cart once again. His mother looked behind her quickly. "Andrew, are you sure you want to go through with this engagement?"

"Father insists upon it, for appearances sake," Andrew said, wishing his mother hadn't brought up the subject. "But if Father still thinks this marriage will change my feelings, then he's mistaken, Mother." Andrew kicked at the stone steps.

"I know, darling. I know all about you and Robert."

"You know about it?" Andrew was shocked but relieved she knew the truth.

"Of course, I do. I've known for a while, but you're my son, and I love you."

"Then talk to Father and get him to change his mind about this wedding and this trip…" Andrew could hear the pleading in his voice.

His mother touched his arm and pulled him closer to her. "I tried, and I don't like this any more than you do. Visiting America with this pair for three months, and then a hurried wedding in August—" She was going to share something else with Andrew, but there was movement and voices in the main hall behind them.

His father returned with William and Claire, her long auburn hair just showing underneath a green felt hat adorned with flowers. Two footmen followed, carrying their trunk between them out to the waiting vehicle.

"Goodbye, sir. Lady Elliot, it's been a pleasure," William said, bowing to Andrew's parents.

"Have a safe journey and look after our Andrew," Lady Elliot said, wiping away a tear.

"We will. I'll make sure he writes every day." Claire smiled, pulling Andrew toward the waiting automobile. Andrew frowned and went back up the steps to his parents. He turned to William and Claire.

"Give us a moment, and I'll be right with you," Andrew waited for the pair to enter the car before he spoke to his parents. Behind him, he heard the car door close, and Andrew stood looking at his parents.

"Don't worry, Mother. It's only three months, and then I'll be home." Andrew smiled cheerfully and gave his mother a hug and a kiss. Frowning, his father stood by, with his hands in his pockets.

"Let's hope this journey to America will restore some sense to you, boy."

"I doubt it and forcing me into marriage with Claire Bennett isn't going to change my mind," Andrew said.

"She's the most eligible girl who has presented herself. She's the daughter of an earl, and I approve of her, my boy, so you'll marry her, or else I'll cast you out without a penny."

"Mac, no—" his mother said.

Sir Elliot lifted his hand and demanded his wife and son stay silent. He looked at his pocket watch. "Let's get on with this goodbye nonsense, or they'll miss the train. Goodbye, Andrew," Sir Elliot said and then turned and went back inside the house.

"Bye, Mother. Please, don't worry. I'll come up with some way to change Father's mind." Andrew smiled. He stepped back and headed to the car.

Andrew glanced alternately at the pages of his book and at the scenery outside the windows of the train as it neared London. Across from him, William and Claire sat with their eyes closed, their heads nodding with the swaying motion of the train. He closed his book, placed it under his arm, and went to the dining car, leaving his companions to nap in the compartment.

A waiter showed him to an empty table, and Andrew waved away his offer of a menu.

"Just a pot of tea and toast would be fine," Andrew said. The waiter bowed and went away, leaving Andrew with his book. Again, he found it impossible to focus, so he closed the book and stared out the window.

In the distance, he saw the turret of an ancient castle that reminded him of his family ancestral estate, Elliot's Acres, just north of Grantown on Spey in the Highlands. It wasn't really a castle but a large manor house. There were ruins in the center of the loch, and if he closed his eyes, he could still see the ancient castle and Robert seated on his horse, riding through the moors behind the

Elliot estate—he looked handsome in his dark brown pants, an open vest, and white shirt. His black hair showed underneath the brim of the cap he always wore.

Robert was the caretaker's son, and at twenty-five, he was just three years older than Andrew. He was tall, tan, and muscular, and his smile could make Andrew melt.

It had been at the beginning of February, on a Sunday afternoon nearly two months ago, that Andrew and Robert had been riding on the moors among the heather. They had gone five miles when it began to rain, and they had to turn around. As the wind and rain increased, they sought temporary refuge in a barn on the edge of the property. After tying up the horses, they sat on a bench, and Andrew remembered Robert's face outlined sharply by an occasional flash of lightning.

Robert smiled at Andrew as he rubbed his hands together and said, "What I wouldn't do for a wee dram of whisky."

Andrew shivered, and Robert put his arm around him, pulling him close. The kiss, when it happened, was exciting and loving, the happiest feeling Andrew had ever experienced. He could still feel it on his lips, still feel Robert's hands sliding through his wet hair.

It was a short-lived moment. During the embrace, they hadn't heard the barn door swinging open on its rusty hinges. Andrew could still see old Mr. Craig as he stood in the doorway, dripping wet, with a harness in his thick hands and a look of anger and disgust on his face.

"Aye, you both better be getting home," he said, brandishing the harness as if he intended to use it on them.

Mr. Craig didn't look Andrew in the face, but the next morning after breakfast, Sir Elliot sent for him.

"You'll be leaving for Edinburgh, and you'll wait until your mother and I have a wee talk with you." He waved his hand at Andrew, dismissing him from his study.

Andrew's thoughts were interrupted by the jarring clatter of wheels over the tracks and the sound of a woman's voice as someone stood over him.

"Andrew, I hope you haven't been waiting for us to eat breakfast," Claire said as she pulled out a chair and sat opposite him.

William came into the car a moment later and joined them at the table. He removed the newspaper he had been carrying under his arm and put it down in front of him. Andrew was going to say something, but the waiter returned with menus for Claire and William, and with Andrew's tea and buttered toast and a pot of jam. The other two ordered breakfast, and when they were left alone, William retreated behind his newspaper while Andrew and Claire spoke.

"Tell me about your aunt and uncle we're staying with in London. Do they live in a grand house?"

"Uncle Angus and Aunt Olivia are my mother's sister and brother-in-law, and I think they have an ordinary London townhouse. I don't know if I would consider it grand or not. You'll see it this afternoon. We'll only be there until the tenth anyway, until we sail for New York." Andrew had his mind on other things, and he wished he could be like William or even his father, who sat at the breakfast table buried behind the paper while everyone else conversed. He thought about the letter to Robert he had started, which was half finished in his pocket.

When the conversation turned to sailing on the tenth, William put down the paper.

"The papers say that this *Titanic* is unsinkable. I was just reading about it. A floating palace, they say," William sounded as if he knew more details about the *Titanic* than Andrew did. To Andrew it was just another passenger liner, a means to get to America. He wasn't looking forward to seven days *at sea* with this overbearing girl and her brother with his beady, cruel eyes.

Claire picked up on her brother's praise of the new liner. "Just think of all the well-known people we'll be surrounded by—John Jacob Astor and his new wife, five months pregnant and only eighteen… the couturier, Lucile Duff Gordon and her husband. The journalist and spiritualist William T. Stead… there will be artists and painters, the cream of society," Claire boasted loudly so everyone around them could hear.

"If you'll excuse me, I want to go back and write a letter," Andrew said, then rose from the table and left Claire and William alone.

Chapter Two

March thirty, 1912 Belfast, Ireland

The sun hadn't risen yet as Matthew Ahearn stepped out of the boardinghouse, his kit slung over his shoulder and the collar of his jacket turned up against the chill breeze that blew off Belfast Lough. He turned to look at the darkened upper story window of the inn. He knew Daniel was still asleep and would not realize that Matthew was gone. He could imagine Daniel waking up with a Guinness hangover and seeing the empty place where he had lain; Daniel would swear and throw his dirty work boots against the wall in anger. He might even search for a note, and finding none, he would go back to sleep.

Matthew thought about it for a few seconds. Even if I go back now, he knew Daniel wouldn't want to talk. He would probably go back to sleep. He probably won't even care that I'm gone.

A mist hung in the air along the waterfront as Matthew walked on. In the gray early morning light from the distant shipyard of Harland and Wolff, he saw the four funnels of the new passenger liner, *Titanic*, outlined against the sky. He knew from talk at the pub where he had worked, and of course from Daniel, that the ship would be leaving Belfast in a few days for her trials and then on to Southampton to prepare for her first voyage across the Atlantic. He and Daniel were supposed to be on that ship, but he would have to go across alone now.

He dug deep into the pocket of his jacket, feeling for the money he'd saved from working at the pub near the shipyards. It would be just enough to get him across to Liverpool and then by train to Southampton, through London.

Having bought passage on a small mail boat, Matthew leaned on the rail as it chugged its way toward the landing stage in Liverpool, England. The men around him ran back and forth to prepare lines and shift bags for unloading, and Matthew was so intent on watching the activity that he was almost thrown off his feet when the boat came alongside the wharf.

Ashore at last, Matthew hurried through the bustle of the docks to the train station and bought his ticket for London. While he waited, he ordered a cup of tea and prayed that he was doing the right thing, leaving home and Daniel for an unknown land.

Monday, April one, 1912 London, England

Matthew had read about London in books, but he wasn't prepared for the reality—streets clogged with people, horse-drawn carriages, and motorcars. And he had only just stepped outside the rail station. A busker was playing an accordion on the corner; he finished playing and held out his cap toward Matthew in hope of a copper or two. Matthew obliged and threw one to him, then walked on.

It was getting dark as Matthew entered a pub on a narrow side street. A man with a tweed cap pulled over his eyes looked his direction and nodded when he passed through the door. The pub was darker and smokier than any place back home in Ireland. In a corner lit only by an oil lamp, a group of men sat playing cards. They eyed him as he walked past and then went back to their game. Matthew sat at the end of the bar and ordered a pint of Bass.

Several hours later, Matthew felt something hard pressing against his back, and his head hurt. He was sitting upright against a brick wall, next to some trash bins, in a dimly lit alley. He looked around and found his bag beside him. A quick search revealed the items he'd packed were still there, but all his money and his continuing train ticket to Southampton were gone.

He remembered sitting at the bar and talking to a mustached man with a worn bowler hat. A woman with a straw hat and long black hair bought them a round of drinks; after that, everything became fuzzy. Someone had obviously drugged the drink. Now he was stranded in London with no way to travel southward. He leaned against the brick wall, struggling to hold back his anger and his tears.

Matthew didn't know how long he sat there with his head in his hands, but a policeman flashed his lamp on him, and then he felt a strong hand grab him by the shoulder.

"You can't sleep here, boy. Get moving," the policeman said.

"I was just robbed back there at that pub," Matthew said, pointing at the doorway.

The policeman scowled. "Let that be a lesson to you not to spend your pay on drink."

"I wasn't," Matthew protested as he got to his feet and picked up his bag. But the policeman only shoved him forward into the street and then continued his rounds.

Matthew stood on the street corner, watching the man walk away.

The first night, he slept under the tattered awning of an East End shop, and in the morning, he spent hours wandering the streets of London, the collar of his jacket turned up against the chill. Once, he caught a glimpse of himself in a window—dirty brown hair and face—and he was glad his parents weren't able to see him broke and hungry.

He could hear Daniel's voice ridiculing him. *See what dreaming gets you, boy? Now what are you going to do?*

Unable to answer, Matthew just walked on through London until his legs were so tired he couldn't walk any more.

Friday, April five, 1912

"Stop, thief! Somebody stop that man, that man with the brown hair and dirty clothes!" A heavyset, balding man in a green apron yelled to the policeman on the corner and appealed to several people who had paused in front of the bakery to see the commotion.

Matthew cradled the loaf of bread under his arm as he rushed into the street. He dodged horse-drawn carriages and motorcars and leaped over a rubbish pile onto the opposite curb. He stopped to catch his breath until he heard the police whistle.

"Stay where you are! You're under arrest!" the policeman ordered, shouting to be heard over the street noise.

Matthew smiled, happy to have outwitted the police, and he started running again, almost tripping over more trash on the pavement. As the whistle sounded closer, Matthew looked over his shoulder. He didn't see the shop door ahead of him swing open and the young man in a derby hat and expensive tweed overcoat preparing to step outside. Matthew had no time for evasion. The man tripped him, and he fell facedown onto the sidewalk, the loaf of bread sliding out of his arms and into a drainage ditch—ruined.

"Are you all right?" the man in the tweed coat asked, offering his hand.

Matthew only looked at the loaf of bread, now covered with mud. He felt as if he was going to faint or cry. He was about to say something to the man when the policeman and the shopkeeper arrived on the scene.

"Come along, you filthy beggar. A few days in jail will teach you." The policeman grabbed Matthew roughly by the arm.

"What has he done?"

The clerk and the policeman turned suddenly, seeming to recognize the young man in the expensive clothes, they both tilted their heads respectfully.

"Beg pardon, m'lord. He walked into my shop, picked up a loaf of my fresh baked bread, and bold as brass took off running." The clerk hissed, wiping his forehead.

The gentleman looked from the clerk to Matthew, who was sitting crouched against the wall under the eye of the policeman and the crowd that had gathered around them.

The policeman stepped toward the man. "I'm sorry to trouble you, Lord Carson, but I can handle it from here." He turned back to Matthew. "Come along, you."

"All this fuss for a loaf of bread. How much does he owe you?" Lord Carson asked.

The clerk looked down at the sidewalk, then back up. "A shilling, but if you ask me, I should charge him a pound for the business I lost chasing him!"

"If it will make you feel any better, here's *two pounds*. That should more than make up for anything." Lord Carson threw the crumpled notes at the clerk.

The policeman let Matthew stand up at last. The crowd, disappointed to see an end to the distraction, began to walk away. The clerk gave Lord Carson a nod and Matthew a sneer, then returned to his shop. The policeman crossed the street, leaving Matthew and Lord Carson alone.

Matthew stared at a crack in the pavement, fingering the frayed brim of his cap. He was aware Lord Carson was still standing there looking at him.

"Thanks, but now that you've done your good deed, you can go back to your posh house and feel better," Matthew said bitterly.

"I was only trying to keep you out of jail." Lord Carson reached over and put a hand on Matthew's arm.

Matthew shrugged it off and took a couple of steps back from his Samaritan. He wanted to run away but felt compelled to stay. *Is it because of his kindness or because he is handsome?*

The silence between them as they stood on the crowded London sidewalk was becoming awkward, so finally Matthew said, "I don't mean to sound like someone off his onion. I don't normally steal from bakers' shops, but I was so hungry, and I was passing by, and it smelled so good sitting there on display with the others. The shopkeeper's back was turned, and I didn't think he'd notice if I hoisted one loaf, so…" He shrugged.

"Come with me. We'll get you something to eat and then see what we can do." Lord Carson moved closer, and for the first time, Matthew was nervous. He smelled whisky on Lord Carson's breath, and even though the man promised something to eat, Carson's eyes suddenly became predatory. Matthew wished he had been arrested as Lord Carson put an arm around him. His lips were near Matthew's ear, and he whispered, "I'll wager you clean up nicely. How old are you?"

"Just twenty, m'lord," Matthew stammered.

"I see. Well, let's have some tea, shall we? Then we'll see what we can do afterwards." Lord Carson led Matthew to a large green-and-black Rolls-Royce limousine parked at the curb. A uniformed man jumped out from behind the wheel to open the door. He scowled when Matthew entered behind Lord Carson, then closed the door behind him.

"Where to, my lord?" the chauffeur asked through the speaking tube.

"The usual place. We'll also stop at the first tea shop we see along the way," Lord Carson said gruffly into the tube. The driver tipped his cap and then started the car.

Matthew sat up in bed. His head ached, and it was cold in the room, so he pulled the threadbare wool blanket around his thin body. Lord Carson was gone, and on the table next to the bed, Matthew saw a half-empty bottle of whisky. Underneath the bottle was a folded pound note. He searched the table in the dim light from the grimy window for any note Lord Carson might have left for him. The only piece of paper was the folded bill.

Throwing the blanket aside, Matthew put his bare feet on the icy floor. He searched for his socks and the rest of his clothing, then dressed quickly. After he'd finished tying his shoes, he stood to look at himself in the small mirror, equally as filthy as the window. His brownish hair was damp from sweat, and his green eyes looked tired. Below the mirror was a pitcher of water, which he used to wash his face before drying it with a towel. Feeling somewhat better, Matthew sat on the bed.

Lord Carson had taken him in his motorcar to a tea shop, where Carson ordered a pot of tea and some food. He'd seemed amused watching Matthew eat.

"I haven't eaten much since I came down here a few days ago… just whatever I could pinch from fruit and vegetable stalls," Matthew had explained.

"How did you manage to find yourself in such a situation, anyway?"

"I stopped for a pint at a back street pub. I was talking to a couple of people, and then I woke up outside, and all my money was gone," Matthew said.

"You're lucky they didn't leave a knife in your back; those places are notorious for such things."

"Anyway, I've been wandering about London ever since, and then I saw the baker's window…"

"Did it ever occur to you to walk into the shop and ask the clerk for a job? Go on and eat, there's more where that came from." Lord Carson pointed at the teapot and plate of sandwiches.

"I'm trying to get to America. I want to be a cowboy, or a rancher just like in the moving pictures or dime novels," Matthew said between bites of food.

"That's an admirable dream. Do you have any experience riding a horse or working with cattle?" Lord Carson couldn't hide his mocking grin. Matthew noticed it but tried to ignore what he saw.

"No, but I've been on a horse, and I can learn the rest." Matthew put aside the cup of tea; he was finished eating. He pushed back his chair and prepared to rise and go his way. "Thank you for the tea, m'lord, but I really have to go now."

"Where are you going?"

"I don't know. Maybe I'll head down to Southampton on foot and try to get a job on that new ship that'll be sailing on the tenth."

"Maybe I can help you get there quicker, lad. And I always like to *help* people." Lord Carson stood up and paid the bill. Out on the street, he led Matthew to the waiting car, and they got inside.

"Where... where are you taking me?" Matthew asked.

Lord Carson smiled at him. "Don't be afraid. I would like you to come with me to a little place I know." He placed a hand on Matthew's knee. Matthew was angry and wanted him to stop, but at the same time, it was kind of exciting. It wasn't every day that a *real life* lord wanted to be with him, so he didn't want to be rude. Yet something about Carson made him nervous.

"If I don't want to do this?" Matthew asked.

"Well, then, I'll turn you over to the police." A shadow of a grin curled Lord Carson's lips.

Matthew pulled out of Carson's grasp, feeling a shiver run down his back. He swallowed hard, his eyes wide with fear.

Realizing the implications of the threat and that Lord Carson could have him charged with anything, Matthew went with him to a hotel not far from the tea shop and followed him upstairs.

The door closed behind them, and Lord Carson dropped his kind façade. He wrapped his arms around Matthew and pulled him close. Matthew found that he was afraid of Lord Carson, whose kiss was wet and sloppy, devoid of passion. He felt a hand moving from his chest to his trousers, fumbling clumsily with buttons and suspenders. Matthew pulled back, but Carson was persistent.

Lord Carson reached into the pocket of his coat and removed a small bottle. "Have a drop of whisky—that might cure your reticence, my boy." Carson took a sip first and then handed the bottle to Matthew.

The liquid burned as it went down, and Matthew almost coughed it up. Carson grinned as he took the bottle and placed it on the bedside table, then pulled Matthew closer.

The act between them was over quickly, and afterward Lord Carson wiped his hands and face with a towel. Matthew reached for the whisky, determined to let the burn of it warm him.

It was going on nine o'clock in the evening, according to a nearby church bell. Matthew was left with a one-pound note and a room that smelled of musk and mildew. He sat on the bed and clutched the flimsy pillow to his face until he pulled it away and discovered he had been crying. He wiped his eyes with his shirtsleeve and sat staring as the room began to get darker. He had no idea how long people were allowed to stay. The innkeeper could come any minute and throw him out. He would have to go.

Matthew finally rose and gathered his bag. He closed the door behind him and walked down the dimly lit hall to the stairs. When he reached the bottom, he paused. A man lay sprawled face down on the landing, probably drunk and passed out. Matthew had to step over the man's left leg to get past him, but as he did so, he stopped suddenly. There was something familiar about the clothes, so he kneeled down to get a closer look, ignoring the strong stench of whisky and sweat. Matthew intended to get the man into a seated position, so he rolled him over. In the faint light, he caught a glimpse of the man's face. Lord Carson—he had apparently fallen down the stairs.

"M'lord, it's Matthew. Are you all right?" Matthew shook his shoulder gently.

He opened his eyes and whispered, "Matthew…"

The gash and the blood almost made Matthew gasp out loud. He collapsed back onto the stairs, stunned. Somewhere a door opened, and he heard footsteps coming down the hall.

In a panic, Matthew stumbled down the steps and ran. He sprinted until his heart pounded loudly in his chest and he could barely breathe. In a small park a few streets away, he had to sit on a bench until the pain in his lungs subsided.

In the distance, he imagined he could hear a police whistle and bells, and they were coming for him. He knew he had to get away from London and make it to Southampton, but all he had was the pound note Lord Carson had left him. Matthew felt drops of moisture on his hand, and he thought it was raining until he realized they were his own tears. Suddenly, footsteps and the light of an electric torch startled him.

"You can't stay here. The park is closed." The voice belonged to a policeman, and for a moment Matthew was afraid.

"I'm sorry…" Matthew said. With relief, he realized the man wasn't there to arrest him, only to ask him to leave. He stood up.

The policeman muttered, "Go home and sleep it off. There's a good lad."

Chapter Three

Saturday, April six, 1912 London, England

Matthew opened his eyes and squinted at the sunlight that came in through lace curtains. He sat up and looked around at the little room in the daylight.

When the policeman had put him out of the park, he'd walked until he found a canteen for the poor run by a local church and staffed by volunteers from the congregation. He received his bowl of thin stew and chunk of white bread, then shuffled to a table. He kept his head down, afraid the police were searching for him and that he would be blamed for harming Lord Carson. Matthew sat in the back of the room, not paying attention to anyone until he felt a hand on his shoulder.

"Move it, mate. This is my place," the burly, bald man in a ragged coat spoke in a deep bass voice.

Matthew pretended not to hear, but the man reached out a rough hand, grabbed him by the collar, and pulled him out of the chair as if he were a feather. Another man, this one with greasy black hair and an ill-fitting coat, stepped toward them.

"Come on, mate, he's just a lad. Why don't you pick on someone your own size, eh?" The burly man let go of Matthew and threw a punch at the one who'd attempted to help. The hit was returned, and the scuffle grew to include several other men. Furniture and bowls were smashed, and above the shouts and screams came the shrill blast of a police whistle. Matthew looked toward the door as it swung open and the police entered. In the distraction, someone hit him on the jaw and knocked him to the floor. He lay there, stunned, until someone picked him up.

The rector of the parish church pulled Matthew from the fight and prevented him from suffering more than a swollen lip. He also prevented Matthew' from spending a night in jail with the others involved in the brawl.

He took Matthew across the street to his house, applied a small chunk of ice to his injury, then guided him upstairs to an extra bedroom.

That's where Matthew woke up the next morning. While he sat on the edge of the bed, there was a knock on the door.

A friendly sounding woman on the other side asked, "Are you awake, lad?"

"Aye..." Matthew said, scrambling into his clothing before he opened the door. The pastor's wife waited outside. Her smile reminded Matthew of his mother, and he felt homesick, especially when she made him sit back on the bed while she looked at the cut on his lip. He flinched when she put a cloth on it.

"It will heal quickly, but you got off lucky, my boy. Big Tom— that's the big man who tried to grind you to mincemeat—a broken nose and sprained wrist is what he got. He'll recover from them after a few days in jail. Now come on down and have some tea." She stood up, and he followed her to the kitchen.

When he finished eating, Matthew was shown into an office where the rector was sitting behind a desk, writing. He looked up and pointed out a chair for Matthew to sit in. The door closed behind him, and they were alone.

Matthew waited, the silence in the room broken only by the scratching of the pen across paper and the ticking of a clock. He watched the rector, wondering what the man was going to say. He didn't have to wait long.

The rector put aside his pen and then looked up at Matthew. "Did you sleep well? Has my wife given you breakfast?"

"Aye, thank you," Matthew said in response.

The pastor sat back and rested his hands on the arms of the chair. Again silence, while outside a horse clomped past the window.

"What's your name, son?"

"Matthew. Matthew Ahearn."

"Do you have a family, Matthew Ahearn?"

"My mother and father died back in November. I have no family *here*," Matthew said before the rector could ask about brothers or sisters.

The man nodded. He picked up the pen from his desk and held it between his fingers. Looking beyond the pen into Matthew's eyes, he said, "What brings you to London, and what made you come to my church last night, eh?"

"Well, sir, I'm only passing through on my way to Southampton."

"Do you have any other family there?" the pastor asked.

"No, sir. I'll be trying to get a job as a steward on that new ship that leaves for America next week. That's the place for me, sir, America." The rector continued to study him over the fountain pen.

"That would be the *Titanic* you're trying to get on?"

"Yes," was all Matthew said, trying not to sound excited, though he did shift in his chair.

"You still have a long way to go before you reach Southampton."

The pastor observed him before he continued speaking, "And because of the coal strike, any positions on the *Titanic* are going to be impossible to come by."

Matthew had thought about that, and he knew that since the miners had been on strike for higher wages, most of the great liners were either cancelling their voyages or crossing at a slower speed to conserve fuel. Many of the working men around Southampton and Liverpool were fighting for space on any ship.

"I have to try, sir. Even if I get a job washing dishes in first class, I'll be aboard."

"When you reach America, what then?" the rector's voice didn't sound encouraging to Matthew, and he hesitated before he spoke.

"I'll work my way to Texas or somewhere West, and find work as a ranch hand," Matthew said.

The rector put down his pen and smiled at him. "Do you have the funds to reach Southampton?"

"I have a pound note." Matthew felt it in the pocket of his trousers, and he could still feel Lord Carson's hands on him. He tried not to let the parson on the other side of the desk see him shiver.

The rector nodded. He reached into his pocket and took out a folded one-pound note.

"This should get you the rest of the way—" A knock at the door interrupted him. "Yes?" the rector called.

His wife opened the door partway. "There's a police inspector outside to speak with you, Thomas."

"Whatever for?"

"He didn't say, but he insists on speaking with you. He says it's important," his wife said.

The pastor stood up. "Wait here until I return," he said to Matthew, and then he stepped outside the office into the receiving parlor.

The policeman was standing with his back to the door, so he didn't see Matthew. But Matthew could hear their conversation.

"How can I help you, sir?" the pastor asked.

"I'm here to inquire about a young man who may or may not have been seen at your soup kitchen last night."

Hearing this, Matthew felt a shiver, but still he continued to listen.

"Countless young men come to my kitchen, sir. It is open to everyone. What has he done, and what does he supposedly look like?"

"Yesterday he pinched a loaf of bread, and later he attacked Lord James Carson at a cheap hotel when Lord Carson tried to help him. That's what he's done. The description I have is that he's less than six-feet-tall, has wavy brown hair and green eyes. He's not armed, as far as we know," the inspector said.

The pastor and his wife, who had remained in the room, were silent. "Is Lord Carson dead, Inspector?"

"No, he's only suffered a nasty bump on the head, but he thinks it's this young lad that pushed him."

"What led you to our little church, Inspector?"

"One of my men thought he saw a young man matching that description last night when he came to put an end to a fight in your soup kitchen."

"Ah, yes, it started because one of my regulars claimed someone was in his seat, but so many people came through our kitchen I can't remember everyone. Only the regulars…"

Matthew listened quietly with his ear to the partly open door. He had to get out of there fast, and the only way out was the window. He crept over to it and worked open the latch, then eased himself slowly over the sill and dropped onto the grass. He held his breath until he was through the garden gate, and halfway down the road, he took off at a run. He didn't look back.

Saturday, April six, 1912 London, England

Andrew sat in a corner armchair, his Aunt Olivia on his right, while his Uncle Angus, William, and Claire sat across the tea table in the drawing room.

"It's wonderful to see you back in London again, Andrew, and with a fiancée. And since you're all here until you sail on the tenth, you and I will have to have a long conversation. Maybe this evening before dinner, or tomorrow we can go for a long walk to Hyde Park," Aunt Olivia said, smiling at Andrew, and he forced a smile in return. His aunt looked from Andrew to Claire.

"Miss Bennett, did you tell me your late father was a Sir Cliverford?"

"His manor was on a small island in the Channel," William spoke up for his sister.

"Which Channel Island is that?" Aunt Olivia asked, lifting an eyebrow.

Claire paused over her teacup and then pointed at a portrait in a heavy gold frame over the fireplace.

"*He looks so much like our late father.*" Tears welled up in her eyes, and she pulled a handkerchief out of her sleeve. William comforted his sister, rubbing her arm.

"It pains her to talk about our family. The fire destroyed all our fine things, *then the old man died of a broken heart* you see. Let's talk about something else," William said.

Andrew and his relatives exchanged uncomfortable glances, and finally his uncle spoke. "So, the three of you will be sailing on the maiden voyage of the *Titanic*?"

"Yes, sir. It was the first available ship to New York," Andrew said. Angus picked up the paper, found the section he was looking for, and read out loud.

"When the White Star Liner *Titanic* leaves Southampton on its maiden voyage on April ten, several well-known names will be on the first-class passenger list. The aide to President Taft, Archibald Butt, the couturier Lucile Duff Gordon and Sir William Duff Gordon, and the Countess of Rothes are among the many well-known people sailing aboard the ship 'God himself cannot sink." Andrew remained silent, he heard the roll of names on the passenger list already.

Andrew listened as his uncle read the remainder of the article, which spoke of all the usual things he had heard about the *Titanic* since the tickets had been purchased. There were elevators, and the very first swimming pool on any liner, a gymnasium, and a Jacobean-style dining saloon, the largest of any such room on a ship, *and even a French sidewalk café with real ivy.* He was looking forward to seeing these wonders in person and writing to Robert about them when he reached New York.

Another cup of tea was poured, and the conversation moved on.

"What are your plans when you reach New York, young man?" Uncle Angus asked between puffs on his cigar.

"I thought we would spend a few days there, maybe see a couple of plays, do some sightseeing and shopping, and then head out west to San Francisco." His uncle remained silent, puffing on his cigar, while Andrew spoke, picturing in his mind stories of cowboys, Indians, and shootouts in Wild West towns that he'd read about in penny novels. "I've always read that the American West is quite beautiful, especially the California coast."

"Interesting," was all Uncle Angus said in response.

"What about the wedding plans?" Aunt Olivia asked.

Andrew sat back and only half listened to Claire's voice and his aunt's replies. He wanted to retreat upstairs and write to his friend, to finish the letter he had started back home, maybe even ask him to come down to London before they left for America.

"Excuse me," Andrew said as he got up and left the room. He went upstairs to his guest room, grateful to shut the door. He leaned on the window frame and looked out, wondering what he could do to get out of this marriage he was being forced into by his father.

His uncle had even taken him aside after their arrival at the train station and said sternly, "You're in my care until the ship leaves for New York, and a word of warning before we reach the house. Your Aunt Olivia knows nothing, except you're coming to visit us until the tenth. You've brought enough shame on our house without making matters worse. In my day, young man, people weren't so lenient with men like you. You would have been put in prison."

"Uncle, this is the second decade of the twentieth century, and if you expect me to blush in shame like a Victorian housewife, you're mistaken. There was nothing wrong with what Robert and I did…"

"There'll be no more of that talk, do you hear me, Nephew?"

"Yes, sir, loud and clear," Andrew had replied. Standing in the bedroom, reflecting on the conversation, Andrew would have loved to have seen his uncle's reaction had he told him that he would rather be with someone, anyone else instead of with Claire. Andrew couldn't suppress a laugh, and he was startled when he heard his aunt's voice.

"I'm happy you still have a sense of humor," Aunt Olivia said through the partly open doorway.

"Aunt Olivia, coming into a man's bedroom, people will be shocked." He laughed, and she joined his mirth.

"I knocked a couple of times, but you didn't seem to hear me. Now, if I was an unmarried woman... However, the rules change for aunts. Now tell me, Andrew, what's going on? Why are you going to America with a fiancé and her brother? Don't lie to me because I know there's something." She sat on the bed, and Andrew sat in a chair across from her.

"I can't tell you, Aunt Olivia. You would be shocked and disgusted if I told you." Andrew felt himself choke up, and he swallowed.

"I've read enough Elinor Glyn novels that I can't be shocked by anything I hear, so now you'll have to tell me. Have you murdered someone or stolen money, perhaps compromised a maid?" Olivia asked.

"No, it's because of whom I chose to..." He paused.

"It wasn't a maid, or else your uncle would have been telling me all about it. Was it a man?" she asked quietly.

Andrew nodded.

His Aunt Olivia turned her head away, pretending to smooth a crease on the bed's coverlet. "I see. That's why your father arranged a marriage with this girl. I don't like her very much, or her brother. They have a ready answer for everything, just like they rehearsed it all. At tea when I asked where they were from, and they spoke about their home and a burned-out estate... I know the island Herm—she mentioned it in our talk about the wedding plans—and I don't recall any *large estate houses* ever being there, and if it was in ruins like she mentioned, then they would have been very prominent, but there was only a small fishing village. Your uncle and I traveled through there a year ago on our way to visit the continent."

"You're very perceptive, Aunt Olivia."

"Enough to see that you're truly miserable. I wish I had some advice that would help," Olivia said, reaching out to put her hand over Andrew's.

"That you understand is sufficient," Andrew said.

"Oh dear," Olivia said.

"I agree. Oh dear," Andrew replied.

Matthew looked up at the stone façade of Waterloo Station before he went in. He glanced to his left and right, and seeing no policemen, he walked up to the ticket window. He reached into his pocket and pulled out the pound notes, one of which the kindly rector had given him before the police inspector arrived.

"Where to, lad?" the ticket seller asked.

"Southampton for one," Matthew said, hoping he had the money. The agent frowned and pulled a slip of paper out of a book.

"One pound six," the agent snapped. Matthew handed him the money and received his ticket and change. There was enough for a room until the ship sailed, and he could spare a little now for tea in the canteen before the train left in thirty minutes.

Matthew took his cup of tea and sat in a corner where he hoped he wouldn't be noticed, where he could watch people come and go through the station. There was a newspaper left on the table next to him, so he picked it up. The coal strike that had been going on for the past few months, caused by miners looking for better wages and working hours, was reaching a settlement. It was still affecting shipping traffic, and Southampton and other shipping towns were facing high unemployment. Matthew prayed he would find a coveted post aboard the *Titanic* when he got there.

On the train, he sat with the newspaper in a corner of the third-class coach and tried alternately to read and sleep, but soon found he could do neither. He was sweating and anxious about everyone who walked by; even an old woman dressed in black and selling flowers to the passengers made him nervous. He didn't relax until he heard the familiar conductor's whistle and the train jerked forward.

Matthew stared out the window, watching as the city gave way to the countryside. He was happy that Lord Carson wasn't dead, but to be suspected of attacking him? Impossible. But they would believe a titled member of the peerage over a twenty-year-old man from Ireland.

He hadn't thought about home much in the five months since his parents were killed in a carriage accident. He'd gone to live in Belfast with Ian, his older brother. Ian worked for the riveting department of Harland and Wolff, the yard where the *Titanic* had been constructed, and Matthew had watched from an upstairs window as construction on the *Titanic* neared completion with the installation of its luxurious interiors and other inner workings. His brother had tried to get him a job at the shipyard, but without any success.

The only job Matthew could get as a newcomer to town was in a pub near the shipyard, pouring whisky and tossing out men who were too drunk to stand. It was because of his job at the pub that one day Daniel had walked into his life. Daniel was muscular and handsome, with curly auburn hair, brown eyes, and a smile that turned the heads of all the young women of Belfast. Matthew discovered his new friend was one of the men working to finish the *Titanic* before its projected sailing date: April 1912.

Daniel came in every day at the end of his shift, and he made Matthew laugh with his jokes. One night after the pub closed, Matthew stayed to lock up and clean, and Daniel sat at a table, watching him as he worked. Finally, Daniel pushed out the empty chair across from him with his foot. Slapping his palm on the table, he said, "Pour yourself a pint of ale and join me, boyo."

After four more glasses of ale, they walked back to the lodging house where Daniel was staying, and upstairs they fell together on the bed. Matthew still remembered that night; he had never been kissed or touched the way Daniel touched him. It was tender and warm, filled with desire, or dare he think it—love?

Matthew closed his eyes and pressed his head against the train window, trying to feel the touch of

Daniel's hand, but the train jerked again, he bumped his head on the window frame, and the newspaper fell out of his hand.

Outside the window, another city came into view as they came around a curve. Over the roofs of distant buildings, Matthew saw cranes, masts, and the funnels of ships that lay at anchor. The train entered a tunnel, and when it emerged on the other side, he recognized the four towering buff-colored funnels with black tops belonging to the ship he had seen close up, the ship everyone was talking about: *Titanic.*

Chapter Four

Saturday, April six to Tuesday, April nine, 1912
Southampton, England

With the last of his money, Matthew found a room in a house near the docks. The room was small and clean, and it smelled of the sea and cooking grease.

"My husband was lucky to get a job on a cargo boat," the old woman who owned the place explained to him. "*There are* so many men out of work. If you intend on getting a job on that new ship, you'll have to clean up. Leave your clothes outside the door, and I'll take care of them while you have a bath—you could do with one." She pointed to the bathroom across the hall and left him to undress.

The dressing gown itched Matthew's body, but he only had to wear it until his clothes, which he could see hanging on the line outside the window, were dry. The woman brought some dinner on a tray and left him without making any attempt at more conversation.

While he ate, he could see three faint wisps of smoke rising from the *Titanic*'s three working funnels. The fourth was for ventilation and to make an impression on the traveling public. Later, when his clothes were dry, he wanted to wander down to the dock and see the *Titanic* completed and ready for her first voyage.

Matthew remembered when Daniel had talked about the ship during his visits to the pub.

"I'm proud to be working on the *Titanic,* even laying carpets in first class, boyo, just to see my work going to sea at last." Daniel had grinned.

"My brother is a riveter. He worked on the *Titanic* too, but the shipyard didn't have any work for me," Matthew said.

Daniel looked at him, shaking his head. "There were so many of us working on her, and I don't mess with the riveters. They're a tough lot."

Daniel had even taken Matthew to the yard as a guest one Sunday afternoon. He'd looked up at the vessel towering in the shipyard and said to Matthew, "We could get jobs on her and go to America, me boy. Haven't you ever wanted to see America?"

"Sure. I have a cousin in a place called Boston, working as a bricklayer…" Matthew hadn't seen his cousin for three years, but the few letters Brian wrote home were always filled with details about life in America—*plenty of jobs going, lots of towns and cities to settle down in and raise a family…*

"You don't sound happy about that, boy. It's a job."

"If I go to America, I want to head West, get some land to farm, or I could be like them actors in the moving pictures," Matthew said, but he instantly regretted telling him because Daniel laughed.

"You're daft, boyo. Stick with bricklaying, and there's more money to be made in reality than in dreams." Daniel had laughed so hard he'd almost fallen off the crate he was sitting on, and Matthew hadn't confided in him again.

Matthew was thinking about the last time they were intimate, seeing Daniel's muscular body standing over him, when there was a knock on his door.

"I'm leaving your clothes on the chair outside the door," the woman said from the other side.

When he opened the door, she was gone. He dressed and left the room, then wandered through the streets of Southampton in the direction of the dock.

It was twilight when Matthew walked past several shipping buildings and warehouses and cranes, and then he saw the ship. It lay at anchor with the stern facing him. The ship that Ian, Daniel, and so many others had worked on for over two years—eight hundred and eighty-two feet long and as tall as an eleven-story building. Four funnels towered high above the sixteen wooden lifeboats that were tied down on deck. On the tip of one of the masts fluttered the Stars and Stripes, the country of her destination, and from another waved the Union Jack, and the house flag of the White Star Line. As he walked forward, he saw the name on the bow in gold letters: *TITANIC*.

Matthew was so lost in wonder at the sight of the ship towering over him that he didn't hear the footsteps walking toward him.

"Grand sight, isn't she, laddie?"

Matthew was startled by the voice, and he turned and discovered it was a policeman. He didn't want the man to suspect he was nervous and was relieved that the policeman wasn't asking his name or if he had been in London recently.

"She sure is a grand ship, sir," Matthew replied. "You wouldn't know if there are any jobs available on board?"

"I wouldn't know about that, but the hiring office is just over there." The policeman pointed to a small building where there was a light on. "Good luck." He patted Matthew on the back and walked on.

Matthew was relieved, but when he opened the door to go inside the building, he was shaking. A man in a navy-blue officer's uniform sat behind a desk, writing something in a book that lay open in front of him. He spoke without even looking up.

"Well, what do you want? It's late," he said curtly, glancing at the clock above his desk without looking at Matthew.

"I was looking to sign on, sir."

"The *Titanic*? Another first-class steward, I'll wager."

"I'll take anything you have open. I'll shovel coal into the boilers.

"I'll—" Matthew was about to go on, but the officer behind the desk looked up and interrupted.

"Hold on, chap. I do have a spot as third-class smoking-room steward. The man who was supposed to take it decided he's superstitious of maiden voyages. Have you ever done this job before?"

"Yes, sir. I worked on the *Lusitania* and *Mauretania*." Matthew didn't like the lie, but it seemed to impress the officer behind the desk.

"I don't suppose you have your wage book?" Matthew searched his pockets, and the officer shook his head.

"Never mind. What's your name and age?" He reached into his desk drawer and pulled out a small book.

"Matthew Ahearn, and I'm twenty, sir." The officer grunted, and he scratched with his pen in the book. He asked for an address, and Matthew gave him the address for the rooming house. The man behind the desk slid the wage book across to Matthew.

"Don't lose this one, Mr. Ahearn. Welcome aboard. Board by the third-class entrance at the stern by nine o'clock Tuesday morning, and report to the chief third-class steward, James Kieran, for your bedding assignment, your uniform, and to familiarize yourself with the ship." He waved Matthew off without a goodbye.

Outside, as soon as the door was closed, Matthew did a little jump, and he couldn't stop smiling and humming to himself as he walked on. *I have a job on the* Titanic, *and I'm going to America!*

London, England

Andrew wasn't able to finish his letter to Robert; there were so many things to do before the tenth. Uncle Angus insisted on inviting several members of the Elliot family who resided in London to the house to meet Claire and congratulate Andrew on his engagement. Andrew tried to be cheerful as Claire held his arm at social functions. He glanced occasionally across crowded rooms at William, who seemed friendly, but there was something about him that Andrew didn't trust—maybe because his family couldn't find any mention of a Sir Cliverford or his family in that matter.

When asked about his family income or his past, William was evasive and would just laugh and say, "Claire and I have more than enough money, so we just drift around Europe, but I suppose we'll settle in Edinburgh after Claire and Andrew are wed."

Andrew tried to smile as his fiancée gushed and showed off the ring. That the wedding was still months away, and that he might learn to love this rather flirtatious woman, didn't bring him any cheer.

Andrew sought an opportunity to speak to Claire or her brother about calling off the trip and the marriage, but at every meal, every visit to an art gallery or play, Claire was making plans and openly discussing them with anyone who would listen to her.

"I saw the wedding dress in *La Mode Illustrée,* or was it *Vogue*? Anyway, it will be simply stunning, and I'm sure everyone will want to copy it," Claire said proudly.

Andrew sat back and listened, and then he said to her, "What about the registry office? That would be just as official as a church wedding."

"Andrew, we have to get married in the church. I'm sure that's what my poor departed father would have wanted. Not a registry office," she scoffed, and Andrew retreated behind his book.

Tuesday, April nine, 1912 London, England

The night before sailing, Andrew's aunt and uncle gave a dinner party at the house as a farewell to the trio, and Andrew found a brief opportunity to have a private conversation with Claire. She was standing alone on the landing, primping herself before the mirror, when Andrew found her. He stood behind her for a minute or two, watching her.

Claire put a final pin in place, and said to Andrew's reflection, "Are you going to stand there and stare as if I were a mannequin?"

"No. There's something I want to say before we go down and before we embark on this voyage. This is the first opportunity I've had for weeks," Andrew said.

"Well, what do you want to say? It must be momentous after all this buildup."

"I agree to this wedding only because of my parents, not because I have any feelings for you, which I don't. I would just as soon back out now, but since we're here, I think there're things about me you should know."

"I know you're a poof. Your father already told me that. We'll work our way past that, and in time, I'll make you forget those disgusting parts of your life."

"I doubt that, and I haven't finished yet…" Andrew caught her by the arm as she pulled away and was preparing to go down.

"Well!" Claire said in an icy voice.

"Until we reach New York, I'll play this little game. I'll walk on deck with you and dine at the same table. I might even try to make friends with your brother, but that's as far as it goes. When we're married, you can live whatever life you're accustomed to. We'll live as husband and wife in name only, a marriage of convenience, I think the term is. It'll all be part of the game, as long as we understand each other," Andrew said.

"Perfectly. Now let's go downstairs, shall we?" Claire said, taking Andrew by the arm.

They walked down together and greeted the guests, and at dinner she and Andrew even laughed together.

Andrew was glad when it was over and he could retreat to the solitude of his room, strip off his tie and celluloid collar, and fall back on the bed. He put his hands behind his head and stared at the ceiling above.

He thought about finishing the letter to Robert, but he couldn't think of anything to say.

The ticking of the clock by his head meant that the hour for the departure for Southampton was getting closer. Andrew sat up when he heard Claire and William talking in the hallway, and he thought William was going to knock—he had done it once before—but they passed by, and two separate bedroom doors closed.

Andrew was glad when sleep finally came at last.

Chapter Five

Wednesday, April ten, 1912

Andrew was impressed by the size of the *Titanic* when he saw the ship for the first time from the window of the boat train. They pulled into the train depot just across from Berth 44, where *Titanic* lay at anchor. William leaned over him, and Andrew caught a faint whiff of aftershave as William pointed out the giant liner.

"That's our ship, Claire." William shifted in the seat, pressing close to Andrew.

"I hope we get luncheon right away. I barely ate anything this morning." Claire yawned. The rest of her words were lost in the roar of steam and the squeal of brakes as the train slowed to a stop.

Andrew felt in his pocket for the tickets. Three first-class cabins—A-17, which was his room, and two adjoining cabins one deck down, B-66 and B-68, for Claire and William.

Andrew helped Claire from the train and let William see to the luggage while they went ahead. Claire stood with Andrew on the pier as he looked up at the side of the ship. She nudged him in the ribs.

"Come on, Andrew. It's not every day we get to sail on the maiden voyage of the most talked-about ship in

England, if not the whole world, and you behave as if you're going to the guillotine."

I am, Andrew said to himself, but he tried to smile and quickly came up with an excuse. "I apologize. I guess I didn't sleep well last night." Andrew stepped out of the way as a steward in a white jacket rushed past him, brushing his shoulder.

"I'm sorry, but I'm sailing, and I don't want to be late," the man apologized as Andrew looked up and met his eyes.

The glance was fleeting as another crewman hurried past, grabbed at his coworker's collar, and called out, "Come on, mate. We have to get back on board or they'll leave us behind."

The man was gone, and Andrew was left staring at the back of a white jacket disappearing into the crowd on the pier side.

"How rude. Probably steerage." Claire scowled.

William arrived on the scene, and together the three of them set foot on the gangplank separating ship from shore. Andrew's footsteps felt like lead as he followed up the gangway and through the doors to first class.

The entrance hall that led into the grand staircase was all oak paneling, white-and black tiled linoleum, and bright crystal light fixtures, with comfortable chairs and potted palms. It was all so beautiful, and everyone was remarking on the decorating, but Andrew gave it a cursory glance and continued on. He didn't even know how he found his way to A-17, but he was inside the room.

"Just press this button under the light switch by the lamp if you need me, sir," a steward said as he showed Andrew where everything was located. The steward opened the door to a wardrobe. When Andrew saw the life belts on the top shelf, he looked quickly away from them and back to the smiling steward. The man placed Andrew's small trunk under the bed and then left him alone.

Andrew unpacked his books and a photograph of his parents, set them on the table next to the bed, and then sat on the sofa. He remembered that earlier in the morning, just before he left his aunt and uncle's home, Aunt Olivia had brought him a letter. He took it out of his pocket and tore open the flap. It was a note from his mother wishing him love and a safe journey, and another letter was enclosed, this one from Robert. With shaking fingers, he tore it open.

Andrew.

Congratulations on your engagement and have a safe journey.

Cordially, Robert.

That was all, one line and nothing about what they had shared, no protest to his upcoming wedding. It wasn't even signed with love; it was signed 'cordially', the kind of closing one might use with someone of slight acquaintance. He crumpled up the letter and threw it across the room, where it bounced and landed in a corner.

Andrew was startled by a sharp blast from the ship's whistle, and he heard a faint hum from deep within the ship as the engines began to turn. He stood up, ran his fingers through his hair, and went out on deck to watch the departure.

Andrew made his way to the rail and looked over the side. There was already an ever-growing space between the *Titanic* and the pier. The sounds of the people on deck and on shore were drowned out by deep blasts from the ship's whistle, and then the *Titanic* began to move forward. He felt someone elbow in next to him and turned to see Claire and William, smiling and waving to the people on land.

Claire nudged Andrew. "We've been looking for you. Come on and cheer up. You're supposed to wave goodbye," Claire said.

"I don't know anybody on the pier." Due to an engagement, his aunt and uncle had decided at the last minute not to see them off on the ship.

"That's not the point. Now smile and wave," William said, lifting Andrew's arm.

Andrew pulled his arm out of his grasp, then smiled and waved mechanically.

Matthew was watching the departure from a porthole in the third-class smoking room until a group of men who had come in early and were already playing cards called out to him across the room.

"Hey there, mate, how about a pint over here?"

Matthew went into the pantry bar to pour ale into four glasses. He looked up when the door opened and his bunkmate and fellow smoking- room steward, Tom, came in.

"Well, we're off, chap, and now our work begins. Where did you say you worked before?" Tom asked, no doubt noting how unsteady Matthew was with the tray.

"The *Lusitania* and then other ships here and there," Matthew said, walking out the pantry door. Tom stepped in front of him.

"Right you are, mate, but didn't they teach you how to carry a tray… and we're not even on the open sea yet. Watch me, and I'll show you how it's done." Tom took the drinks from him, and Matthew followed, watching how he balanced with the slight rise and fall of the deck. Tom watched Matthew walk across the room, and he laughed out loud. He gave the tray back to Matthew and observed as Matthew walked over to the table.

"We'll make a sailor of you yet," Tom said.

Matthew passed around the ale to his passengers, pausing to look briefly over his shoulder to see Tom staring at him. *Is he watching how I handle people?* Matthew ignored him and went back to his work.

Matthew thought Tom was no comparison to Daniel, but he was nice-looking and friendly. Just before they sailed, Tom had even snuck off the ship with

Matthew for a pint of ale at a nearby pub, and they had run back to the ship before they were missed. It was on the dock that he remembered seeing the handsome chap with the red hair curling underneath a derby hat. When their eyes had met and held, he'd noticed the man's eyes were green. Matthew felt a spark between them that was lost when Tom had come running up to hurry him onboard. Matthew could still picture the man's face in his mind.

While Claire and William went down for lunch, Andrew remained at the rail until the *Titanic* was away from the docks, out of Southampton waters, and began to pick up speed past the Isle of Wight into the English Channel toward her next port of call, Cherbourg, France.

There was a little anxious excitement on departure, Titanic size and forward movement pulled another ship tied up nearby from its moorings. It seemed like both ships would collide, but at the last minute, Titanic slowed, and a tugboat nudged the smaller ship out of the way. They were on their way toward open water again.

Andrew remained at the rail for a while longer, as England receded into a faint mist behind the ship.

Then he returned to his cabin and read until the light outside his frosted glass window grew faint. He laid aside his book and realized it was time to get ready for dinner. He dressed quickly.

Andrew found Claire and William at the foot of the grand staircase, looking up toward the clock that symbolized honor and glory crowning time. William was the first to see Andrew as he approached.

"There you are. We were about to send a search party," William teased.

"No need for that. I was reading and lost track of time," Andrew said, and just then a steward in a white jacket passed by. Andrew remembered the young man with the white jacket he'd seen on the pier.

"Well, it's good to see you smiling," Claire said, taking his arm and leading him down to the dining saloon.

The string orchestra was playing selections from *Cavalleria Rusticana* near the entrance to the dining saloon as they walked in. Andrew, Claire, and William shared a table with the artist, Frank Millet, who was planning to visit the American West, and William T. Stead, who evoked laughs from everyone when he promised not to tell any of his ghost stories while Claire was at the table. While they were settling back in their seats, a gentleman walking past the table recognized Mr. Stead and stopped to shake his hand.

"Mr. Andrews," Mr. Stead addressed the man. "May I introduce Andrew Elliot and Claire and William Bennett." Mr. Stead smiled. "Thomas Andrews here designed the *Titanic*, and a wonderful job he did too."

Claire and William nodded.

Andrew took the opportunity to say, "Mr. Andrews, this is a truly magnificent ship. You must be very proud."

"Indeed, I am, Mr. Elliot. Thank you." Thomas Andrews looked as though he intended to say something else to Andrew in response, but a gentleman walked up to him.

"I'm sorry to disturb you, Mr. Andrews, but there's a problem with a fan on F-deck, and the engineer would like you to take a look at it with him." The man left.

Thomas bowed to Andrew and the rest of the table. "If you'll excuse me, it appears I'm needed somewhere."

"Always in demand, eh, Mr. Andrews?"

"By the *Titanic*, my friends. Where my ship is concerned, I'm at her beck and call." Thomas Andrews turned and walked out of the room. Andrew was seated next to Frank Millet, and the two struck up a conversation.

"I saw a photograph of one of your paintings in an art publication recently, Mr. Millet. I believe the title was called *Wandering Thoughts*, very true for those of us who find our minds drifting during church services. I wonder what was on the young lady's mind."

"That could be a matter open to much discussion, Mr. Elliot. Perhaps she's thinking about a lover, or perhaps it's the burden of the duties life has sent her that I was invoking in her reverie. I'm happy you like the painting," Mr. Millet said.

Andrew nodded. "Anyway, sir, I really would love to see the painting up close instead of in the pages of a magazine—"

"I've always wanted to become an artist," William suddenly interrupted Andrew.

"Please, William, if you had it your way, you would lounge all day and sketch apples in ugly bowls. There can't be any money in such things. Not to say you don't make any money on your work, Mr. Millet," Claire said.

Andrew and Mr. Millet exchanged glances, then went back to their conversation concerning art and chess.

"I do play chess, Mr. Millet. Perhaps we can play this evening after dinner, or at the first opportunity," Andrew said. While he spoke to Mr. Millet, he could see from the corner of his eye that Claire and William were looking at him over the appetizers. They didn't seem very pleased to be ignored by the rest of the table. They only smiled and joined in when a question was aimed at them; otherwise, they ate in silence.

There was another tense moment at the table during the second course when a middle-aged woman in bronze velvet walked by on the arm of a gentleman. The woman looked at Claire as if she was trying to place her, and then she stopped.

"Excuse me, but have we met before? In Cairo, *October*, I think it was, on a visit to the Sphinx," she said.

Claire looked flustered, glanced quickly at William, then looked back at the lady. "I don't think so. I've never been there…"

"I'm certain you were, *or perhaps London recently?* I don't forget faces."

"Perhaps it was Paris. I'm there so often, you know," Claire replied, but she was taken aback when the woman addressed her in French, asking if she was enjoying the voyage. Claire didn't respond but only looked down at her gloves, over interested in a button.

The woman and her escort finally walked away. The others at the table let the incident pass, but Andrew sat over his beef consommé spoon in hand. He had caught Claire in a lie. When Claire and William had first arrived as guests at his parents' home, they had both mentioned being in Egypt prior to arriving in London and Scotland, and anyone traveling through Paris might know basic French. He felt someone lightly touch his arm.

"You looked like you were on another world over there, Andrew, and your soup is getting cold," Claire said.

"I'm sorry," Andrew replied.

"You're improving, boy. I don't know what they taught you on the *Lusitania*, but you'll be a steward yet," Tom said from behind as Matthew carried a tray with glasses of ale toward another table of cigar smoking cardplayers. He reminded the men that the smoking room closed at eleven thirty, in twenty minutes, set the drinks down, and turned to see Tom still standing in the doorway to the pantry. Tom looked quickly away.

Matthew returned to the pantry and found Tom washing glasses and putting them up in a cupboard. Tom put the last one away and shut the door.

"I can't wait for this day to be over, mate. Fancy a smoke after we're done?" Tom patted the pocket of his white uniform jacket.

"We won't get in trouble?"

"No. We'll be off duty, so they can't say anything," Tom assured him.

"Sure, I'll join you." Matthew smiled.

Andrew sat up in his bed reading, listening to the faint throbbing of the engines. He thought about finishing the letter he had started writing to Robert a few days earlier. The pages were stuck in the back of the book he was reading. Unable to read or sleep, he closed the book and set it aside. He got dressed and went for a walk.

Except for himself and a lone crewman washing down the deck, it was deserted. Andrew pulled on his tweed cap and walked to the end of the first-class section, which looked over the second and third-class space at the stern. He tried to think about Robert, but every revolution of the propellers took him farther away and into an unknown future.

Andrew tried not to think about Claire and her brother, but they hung about his neck like an anchor. Tomorrow the *Titanic* would make a final stop in Queenstown, Ireland. It would be so easy to slip off the ship with disembarking passengers, and they would be out on the open sea before his absence was discovered. He looked above him at the millions of stars, and then the squeal of a door on its hinges below compelled him to look down.

Two men appeared in the square of light, and Andrew saw their white jackets. *Stewards off-duty?* Before the door swung closed behind them, Andrew caught a quick glimpse of a face in the light. The man was young, and his hair was wavy and maybe a little too long. Then the young man lifted his head and looked up. Andrew was sure they locked eyes for a second.

He saw the shadows as the two men walked to the rail. There was the flash of a match lighting up their faces as they lit cigarettes. They stood there for a few minutes before one of them moved away and went inside, leaving the other still at the rail.

A sudden gust of wind blew around Andrew, and it caught the cap he was wearing. He tried to catch it, but it flew just beyond his reach, sailing over the railing.

Matthew was leaning against the rail, smoking, when he felt something hit him gently on the shoulder and fall at his feet. He bent down, and in the dim light, he saw a man's cap. He looked around to see if anyone was nearby, but there was nobody until he heard footsteps. A man came down the steps from first-class. Matthew couldn't see his face at first.

"You've found my cap," the man said, reaching out his hand.

"How do I know it's yours? Somebody else could have lost it," Matthew said, keeping it just out of the man's grasp as he stepped into the light. Suddenly Matthew's heart was beating fast.

"It's brown tweed, which of course you can't tell in the dark, but it has a tag with the name Lock and Company Hatters, St. James Street, London on the inside... here." The man grabbed the cap and showed him the telltale tag under the dim light of a nearby lamp.

When the man lifted the cap, their fingers touched for a second, and Matthew felt a rush of static electricity through his body.

"You're lucky it didn't go overboard," Matthew said.

The man was about to speak, but a door opened, and bright light illuminated them as a sailor came out. The man stepped back.

"Thank you for rescuing my cap," the stranger said, and then he turned and went back up the stairs.

Matthew remained standing in the same place, watching him until he slipped over the rail to first class and was gone.

Matthew returned to the stewards' quarters on E-Deck that he shared with Tom and several other stewards from third-class. Tom whispered to him across the space between their bunks.

"The morning comes pretty quickly, mate. Better get some sleep."

"I stayed to finish my cigarette and get some air," Matthew whispered back. He heard Tom grunt and roll over.

Matthew got undressed and climbed under the blanket, but he lay awake, staring up at the springs of the bed above him. He thought first about Lord Carson. *Surely he can't blame me for his fall down the stairs? That was due to his clumsiness.* Then there was the cap between his fingers, and the dimly lit face of the young man who came to retrieve it; the man's face was etched into Matthew's mind—young, with red hair and green eyes, square jaw. It had been too dark to tell what kind of a body he possessed beneath the overcoat, and Matthew didn't even get a name to go with the face. All he'd found out was the name of the hatmaker. He pressed his head back into the pillow and closed his eyes.

Claire sat at the dressing table brushing her hair, the usual one hundred strokes. William lay on his back on the bed, using one of his fingers to balance a fountain pen. Suddenly Claire slammed down the hairbrush, the pen clattered on the floor.

"Will you please stop that, now sit up like an adult and talk to me." She swiveled around to face him. William placed his feet on the floor, pressing his hands together so angelically that Claire suppressed a smile.

"Go ahead, Claire, you were saying."

"I wish this wedding had taken place before we left England. Then we'd have the money and be on our way to America, Andrew and his family would still be at the church wondering what the hell happened."

"In the meantime, we have to keep up the charade." William sighed sliding off the edge of the bed, moving to the sofa behind Claire. She shifted her seat to face him.

"Yes, I'm just thankful that woman didn't make a scene in the dining saloon tonight."

"This ship is only so big, she'll gossip." William sat with his chin resting on his hands. Claire swiveled in her chair to face him, and shrugged, smiling.

"That'll be tiresome of course, but it's going to be in her best interest to keep quiet." Claire moved the brushes and combs around on the dresser. Her brother watched in silence; she spoke again after a minute of thought.

"It's her husband that old fool, following us around Cairo, and to London. If she hadn't walked into the salon, red in the face and confronting me in front of everyone, I would have an entire Lucile wardrobe, shoes, and jewelry, instead of the one dress." She pointed to the closet where the dress hung. "Damnation."

"Well, don't worry, darling, all that will happen soon enough."

"I'll have to learn a few phrases in other languages," she added as an afterthought. "I shouldn't have mentioned Paris, but it was the first thing I thought of, besides St. Petersburg."

"That's ambitious." Her brother chuckled. Claire fell silent, the only sound was the ocean, the faint throb of the engines, and light music from the lounge above.

"Right now, we have to focus, Andrew may be getting suspicious."

"Well, we're in the middle of the Atlantic, he can't do much, and we'll take care of it if he says anything." William smiled a little and Claire nodded.

Chapter Six

Thursday, April eleven, 1912

Andrew woke, bathed and dressed before dawn, and sat over his book in the reading and writing room, which was where William found him.

"Good morning, Elliot old chap. Fancy a walk before breakfast?" William said, reaching out to touch Andrew's arm. His hand lingered there, and Andrew pulled away. William frowned.

Andrew closed his book and got up. He followed William out of the room and across the lobby of the grand staircase out to the promenade. A few other early risers wandered about, and Andrew greeted them as he and William passed by.

"What's on your mind, Andrew? You don't often say much. It's hard to tell what you're thinking. You're a strange duck. I wish I understood you."

"I don't really want to talk about it, at least not at this minute," Andrew said as they walked on ahead.

"Well, I hope it's nothing that will spoil your and Claire's future life together. I would hate for that to happen," William said.

Andrew looked sideways at him. "William, about your sister…"

"Is this about last night's incident in the dining room? Well, we've never seen that woman, and we've never been to Egypt. I don't know why she was trying to make a scene," William said.

Andrew didn't answer him. He wasn't thinking about last night's episode, though he could guess the truth about that. He was thinking about his brief encounter with the young crewman—he wished he knew his name so he wouldn't have to keep thinking of him as 'the young crewman' forever.

As he and William continued their walk, they drew near the same spot where he'd stood the evening before and caught his first glimpse of the man; soon they were at the spot and about to pass it by. Andrew saw a door down the well deck open, and several steerage passengers came through, followed by two stewards. One of them looked familiar, even in the daylight.

Andrew leaned forward over the rail to see if he could catch a glimpse of the man's face, and for a second, the steward turned to look in Andrew's direction.

It was *him*. Andrew's heart suddenly began to beat quicker. He felt a tight grip on his arm at the same time.

"What's wrong with you, old man? There's nothing to see down there except third-class passengers and some crew. Nobody to interest us, I'm sure," William said.

The steward and his companion were gone as quickly as they'd appeared. Andrew straightened up.

"Come on, Andrew, let's go find Claire. I'm sure she's looking for us," William said as they walked away from the rail. Andrew really didn't want to leave, but William pulled him along by the arm, and Andrew turned to glance quickly over his shoulder as they moved away.

Matthew and Tom came out onto the well deck, and Matthew happened to look up. He saw the shape of a cap and a face he would know even in the daylight.

Tom nudged him. "Come on, mate. We've got work to do. We arrive in Queenstown after eleven o'clock, and then we'll get the Irishmen in here, and we'll have our work cut out for us." Tom pulled Matthew by the sleeve of the jacket into the doorway leading to the third-class smoking room.

While they were cleaning up and preparing for their day, which would begin after breakfast, Tom spoke softly to Matthew as he was wiping down a table, "You should be careful. If the chief steward finds out or catches you, it could mean trouble."

"I don't quite get your meaning, but it sounds like you think I was meeting someone on deck after dark."

"I don't think anything of the kind, mate. Did you meet someone?" Tom asked, and Matthew warily looked around him.

"A passenger who lost something and came looking for it. I returned it, and he went away." Matthew shrugged, and Tom didn't seem impressed. He turned away and went back to polishing glasses stacked on a sideboard.

Matthew went about his work, but he could feel Tom's eyes on him. He tried his best to ignore it, looking for an excuse to take a second to go outside and see if a handsome gentleman in a tweed cap was standing at the rail looking down.

During a free moment, Tom spoke to Matthew again, "Look, Matthew, I'm your friend, even if I haven't known you long, and I'm on your side. Don't get involved with passengers. It's an ironclad rule. They get off the boat at the end of the voyage, and you never see them again."

"I'm not getting involved with anyone, Tom, believe me. If I was, I would say hang the rules," Matthew insisted.

"Okay, mate, take it easy," Tom said.

"I'm sorry, mate. I didn't mean to snap," Matthew sighed. Tom smiled and patted him on the back in understanding.

The door to the smoking room opened, and a group of men entered and seated themselves on the

benches along the wall.

"No rest for the wicked, mate. Let's go," Matthew said, stepping toward the passengers as Tom followed.

William and Andrew were still out walking when Claire stepped on deck and came toward them. Under her arm she carried copies of *Vogue* and *Le Mode Illustrée*, which she showed off hurriedly and then tucked under her sleeve. William took her arm, and the three of them continued strolling together. Andrew barely heard the conversation between the other two. He was thinking about the crewman, until Claire paused at the railing and pointed into the distance. The Irish coast began to appear out of the mist. Andrew stood watching it grow clearer every passing moment, and his reveries were quickly broken by a tug on his arm.

"Come along, you two. All harbors and tenders look alike. Let's go down to luncheon," Claire said, backing away and clutching at Andrew and William.

"You go down, and I'll catch up," Andrew said, hanging back from them. William shrugged, and Claire gave him a faint smile. He watched them walk away.

Andrew was on deck alone when the *Titanic* made its turn and dropped anchor off the breakwater of Queenstown, Ireland. He watched as two small boats chugged toward them from the shore, carrying passengers and mail. He still had the letter to Robert tucked away in the pages of his book, but it would be too late before he finished it and gave it to someone to take ashore.

The boats were moving closer now, and he could see people eagerly looking up toward the ship. The gangway doors were open and ready to transfer passengers and mail. He wanted to make his move, but his feet wouldn't let him.

"If I leave the ship now, then I'll never find out who the young steward is."

"What's that, old man?" William asked. Andrew turned around from the rail.

"Nothing, just thinking out loud."

"Well, Claire is waiting for us in the dining saloon. Shall we join her?" William asked.

Andrew nodded, realizing that there was no escape now. He walked with William into the dining saloon and over to the table where Claire sat.

"Look who's joining us at last," Claire said as Andrew pulled out his chair and sat.

While they were sitting over their coffee and waiting for the food to arrive, Andrew silently studied the design on the saucer in front of him. He was thinking that he had been bold enough to chase after his cap the night before. *But do I dare go down there to third-class in search of him?* He was snapped to attention by a gentle tug on his sleeve.

"Andrew, may I introduce the Countess of Rothes and her cousin, Miss Cherry," Frank Millet said.

Andrew smiled and stood. "It's a pleasure to meet you, Countess, Miss Cherry."

"And you, sir," the Countess said, smiling, before her cousin pointed out someone who was waiting for them nearby. They nodded graciously to Andrew and the others, then walked off.

Out of the corner of his eye, Andrew saw Claire and William exchanging clouded looks and whispering. He sat and sighed, wishing he could stand up and go down to third-class to find the young man.

After their meal, Andrew, Claire, and William went up on the boat deck for a walk. The *Titanic* was preparing to weigh anchor and begin the rest of her journey to New York.

The trio walked along, with Andrew guiding them to the same familiar spot, hoping that somehow, he might catch a glimpse of the young man.

The *Titanic* was now heading west off the coast of Ireland; ahead was the wide-open ocean. Matthew excused himself from his duties long enough to watch the Irish coast fade away in the distance.

Who knows when I'll see it again?

He blinked back a tear and was going back inside when he looked up, and *he* was there at the rail, looking down at Matthew. Next to the man, he saw another young man and a woman in a large, feathered hat. He felt his heart pounding in his chest, and he couldn't resist the urge to smile and wave.

Andrew couldn't believe his eyes when he saw the steward down there. The man lifted his hand, perhaps to wave.

"Look, I think that steward is waving at us," Claire's words sounded like an invective.

"He should confine his eagerness to his own class. Thank heaven, our steward wouldn't lower himself to do *that*!" William clutched his chest in horror.

Andrew had to suppress a laugh. He didn't care what the man did for a living; he would rather get to know him, instead of judging his work. When William pulled him away from the rail, Andrew looked over his shoulder and saw the young steward still looking up. He managed only to smile before William and Claire dragged him away.

"Why do we want to keep watching the Irish coast? It looks the same as any other. Let's see if we can get a fourth for bridge," Claire said. Andrew quickly glanced back, but the young steward was gone.

Andrew wasn't too interested in playing bridge, and the young woman William and Claire had recruited to be his partner constantly tapped her fingers on the table and was impatient when it took him too long to make a play.

"You already called no trump. Would you keep your mind on the game, please!" she said brusquely.

"I'm sorry, but I was thinking about something else," Andrew apologized and played his cards. He sat back and tried to focus on the game, but he kept waiting for a chance to slip away. He wished the hands on the clock would move faster and the bugler would sound the call to prepare for dinner. While everyone was dressing, he would get down to the stern well deck the same way he had done to fetch his cap.

His companions looked at him impatiently until he focused once again on the card game.

The door to the lounge opened, and a stout, middle-aged woman with wisps of hair escaping from under the brim of a large, plumed hat came in. She called out greetings to people she knew and took her place with a man and another woman at a table next to Andrew. She smiled at him warmly and then turned to converse with her friends.

Claire leaned over her cards and said into Andrew's ear, "That's Mrs. Margaret Brown. Some people call her Molly. She's new money, and I would hate to think of how she and her husband earned their bread in the past." Claire sniffed.

Andrew remained silent, wishing the hand of cards was over. Finally, he put his cards aside and got up from the table. He exchanged another smile with Mrs. Brown, then excused himself from his companions and went on deck.

With the door to the lounge closed behind him, Andrew allowed himself to relax.

He preferred reading, writing, or playing chess, even though William poked fun at such pursuits, *saying that he preferred hunting and cricket*. Andrew shook his head, trying to rid himself of any thoughts of William, but they didn't go away this time. He felt uncomfortable with the way William stared at him. William always looked as if he were plotting some scheme, and then there was the incident at Andrew's parents' home.

It had been the evening his father had announced Andrew would marry Claire. There was much initial celebration, even though Andrew wasn't happy. Later that night, after the house had gone to bed, Andrew had just pulled the blankets over himself when he heard a soft knock on his bedroom door.

He got out of bed, thinking it was his mother or father coming to talk to him once more, but when he opened the door, he found William leaning on the doorframe, grinning.

"What do you want, Mr. Bennett? I'm getting ready to go to bed."

"That's splendid, my boy. That's what I was hoping," William said, pushing Andrew back into the room and closing the door.

"Get out of here, or I'll call out for the butler," Andrew said, standing his ground before William.

"No need for that, old man. I thought I would come and see if you were up for a little company. It's a cold night."

"It's early spring, and there is a fire in the grate, in case you haven't noticed," Andrew said, pointing out the fireplace to one side. He took a step back, and William followed.

"So, there is, but I know what will make this room warmer," William said. He grabbed Andrew and kissed him.

The kiss lasted only a few seconds before Andrew pushed him off. He was preparing to put William out when a knock sounded on the door.

"Who is it?" Andrew called.

"It's Michael, sir. I heard a noise. Are you all right?" The butler, Michael, had been making his night rounds before retiring. Andrew had never been happier to have Michael knock than at that moment.

"I'm fine, Michael. I knocked over a chair in the dark," Andrew said, with a stern look at William.

"Very good, sir. I'll be going up now, if you don't mind?"

"Good night, Michael," Andrew said.

Michael bid him good night in return, and they heard his footsteps fading away down the hall.

When they were alone again, Andrew opened the door and looked out. The coast was clear. He held the door open wide for William. "Now get out, and I'll not mention this to my father in the morning."

"Okay, but after you're married to my sister, you'll come begging me for it, old man." William chuckled.

"Don't hold your breath waiting." Andrew pushed him into the hall and tried not to slam the door. Before he closed it, however, he pulled William back and said, "Since we have to appear together in public from now on, I'll play your little game and be cordial, but don't expect me to be your best friend."

William had smiled smugly, shrugged, and walked away.

Pushing aside the memory, Andrew walked along the promenade deck, wishing he had left the ship in Ireland.

Now he was trapped.

Chapter Seven

Andrew stood at the end of the first-class deck. His gaze alternated between the Irish mountains receding into the misty distance behind the *Titanic*, and the doors leading to the third-class public rooms, as he hoped for a glimpse of the handsome steward. He waited ten minutes until the coast was clear, and then he climbed over a ladder, crossed a deck, and went down another ladder to the third-class well deck.

Two sailors working on some gear saw him, and one of them addressed him. "Sir, you shouldn't be down here. This is for third-class only," the man reprimanded.

Andrew kept walking. "I know, but I won't stay long, and I'll do my best to behave properly." He left the two sailors behind. In front of him was a wide stairway going down. On either side of that, there were doors, one leading to the general room and the other to the smoking room. He tried the door to the smoking room.

When the door closed behind him and he stood in the doorway, several men looked up from checkers and cards to stare at him before returning to their games. Andrew didn't see any stewards. Disappointed, he was about to leave, when a side door opened, and *he* came out carrying a tray with glasses and a bowl filled with something Andrew couldn't see.

Matthew stopped and almost dropped the tray. He would recognize that cap and the man smiling at him anywhere. He only moved when Tom spoke from behind him.

"What's wrong with you, mate? You're in my way!"

"Sorry…" Matthew stuttered, walking to the table where the passengers waited. He could barely keep his eyes off the handsome stranger, afraid lest he look away and the man would be gone.

Matthew passed around the glasses of ale and the bowl of nuts, then went to where the man stood by the entrance.

"I came to thank you for saving my cap." The man smiled, pointing to his head.

Matthew blushed. "You thanked me last night, but you shouldn't be down here," he said, trying not to sound too nervous or excited.

"I thought it's only steerage that wasn't allowed in first class, not the other way around, but I wanted to find you."

Matthew was ecstatic when he heard that, but he could feel Tom's eyes on them. "You could get us both into trouble…"

"There's no harm in having a pint of ale and a cigarette, is there?" The man took a seat on one of the benches.

"I guess there isn't, but it's not your place to be down here. You belong up there with the nobs," Matthew said, pointing toward the first- class decks.

The man remained sitting. "Not until I get my glass of ale and your name. I'm Andrew Elliot." He pulled a case of cigarettes from his pocket, lit one, and blew the smoke over his head.

Matthew leaned forward toward Andrew's ear and whispered, "I'm Matthew, and I'll bring you a pint, but then you have to go."

"I promise faithfully to flee the ball when my time's up."

Matthew turned and walked to the pantry. He almost jumped, not expecting to find Tom waiting for him behind the door.

"Who's that passenger you're talking to, mate?"

"Nobody… Just some first-class passenger who came down here wanting a drink."

"Did you remind him that he's not allowed down here?"

"I did, but he insists on staying," Matthew said, opening the door to the storage room where ale and other spirits were kept. He removed a bottle and poured some ale into a glass while Tom went on.

"You ought to insist that he leave. His kind belongs up in first class with the rest of them. If you won't tell him, mate, then I guess I will," Tom spat, and Matthew stopped him before he got out the door.

"All right, I'll tell him." Matthew pushed past Tom and walked empty-handed over to where Andrew was sitting.

"Please, I'm going to have to ask you to leave. I would love you to stay, but you don't belong down here any more than I should be up there," Matthew said.

Andrew sat back for a moment, arms folded, looking at Matthew. Their eyes locked on each other. "I'll go for now, but I promise I'll come back, and we can have a real talk. I don't suppose you have time off?" Andrew said, rising from the bench and taking a few steps.

"Only for meals and after we close up here," Matthew told him.

Andrew frowned and looked at his pocket watch. "Then goodbye for now, Matthew." Andrew walked away, and Matthew watched the door close behind him.

Outside on the deck, Andrew stood motionless. A couple of sailors and a woman strolling past with a little boy in tow glanced at such a well- dressed man in their space and then quickly passed by. Lifting his head and seeing the lights of first class, Andrew made a move to go back, but he hesitated.

I've come this far to see Matthew. I can't just walk away...

Andrew turned around and went back into the smoking room. Seeing him across the room, Matthew stopped what he was doing.

Matthew wanted to frown to discourage Andrew, but instead he was glad to see him, and Tom was busy in the back. He pointed to an empty place.

"I didn't get my glass of ale." Andrew smiled, removed a pound note from his pocket, and put it on the table in front of him.

Matthew leaned over to whisper, "I ought to insist you leave, but now you're here, I…"

"Have to bring me what I want, and maybe you can spare a minute to talk."

"I think I can." Matthew scanned the room, but everyone was involved in games or conversations for the moment. Matthew nodded, went in the back to get Andrew's drink, then returned with a glass of ale.

"Thank you," Andrew said after he took a sip, then looked up and met Matthew's eyes.

"Is this your first trip to America?" Matthew asked after searching his mind for something to say.

"Yes," Andrew replied with some bitterness, then softened his tone and continued. "We'll be in New York for a week or two and then travel west to Chicago, Saint Louis, Denver, San Francisco."

Matthew smiled; he was familiar with the places Andrew mentioned from the penny novels he read.

"What are you thinking about?" Andrew asked.

"I was thinking—" Just then, from a nearby table, a group of men called for Matthew to get them a round of drinks. Matthew acknowledged them, and walked away.

The moment between Andrew and Matthew had ended.

Andrew downed his ale, and with a final nod and smile at Matthew, he left the room.

Matthew went to the pantry, shut the door, and sat on a stool. Tom came in with a tray of empty glasses.

"What's the matter with you?" Tom asked.

"Nothing is the matter." Matthew remained sitting. He wanted to tell Tom that he was happy Andrew had come down to look for him, and he wished he could have stayed longer, but he didn't want trouble.

Matthew finally stood up, quickly poured the glasses of beer and whisky for his passengers, then picked up the tray and exited the room.

William and Claire, who were already sitting down at the dining room table when Andrew arrived, didn't question his absence during the rest of their card game.

"You look happier this evening than I've seen you in a long time," William observed, studying Andrew's face.

Andrew quickly averted his gaze down to the menu and said without looking up, "I think this trip will turn out to be just grand, after all."

"Are you up for another game of cards after dinner?" Claire asked hopefully, only to pout when Andrew shook his head.

"I'm sorry, but I promised to play chess with Mr. Millet afterward," Andrew said.

"You look a little like you've been hit by Cupid's arrows." William leaned in close to whisper so only Andrew and his sister could hear.

"I wouldn't go as far as to say that, but suppose I have," Andrew returned.

"Then your attitude toward marrying my sister has changed. Your father will be happy to know that." William smirked.

"Come on, you two, stop bickering and enjoy your dinner," Claire said to them.

After dinner, the three of them went out into the palm room for coffee and to listen to the orchestra present an after-dinner concert of *light classical music*. Halfway through the concert, Andrew excused himself and went upstairs to the boat deck. He clung to the ropes latching down one of the lifeboats and stared downward at the waves that swept away from the side of the ship.

In the foam, he imagined he saw the faint image of Robert's face carried farther and farther away with every revolution of the propellers. He saw his home and his comfortable life with his family, his mother and father, his books, being erased and replaced with a woman he didn't love, filled with airs and graces that sounded as if they were pulled line by line from a cheap novel. Andrew saw her brother with his bristling moustache and grating manners, and he shut his eyes.

When he opened his eyes, he could still faintly hear the orchestra playing some romantic piece he recognized as *Musetta's Waltz* from *La Bohème,* which he had once seen in London with his aunt and uncle. The sweet melody of the violins made him smile and think about Matthew, and the reason he remained on board the ship. He stepped back and let go of the rope, then stepped along the boat deck, the music trailing faintly behind him.

Andrew looked down over the rail toward the steerage spaces at the stern. There were lights on in the smoking room, and he could easily imagine Matthew in his white jacket, carrying pints of ale.

Andrew could just see his father's face if he knew Andrew was thinking about a fresh-faced young man with bright eyes, one who waited tables. His father's disapproving gaze and the presence of Claire and William in his life interrupted Andrew's thoughts for a brief second, but he pushed them out of his mind. He stood at the rail for a few minutes before he realized he wasn't alone. Mr. Millet and Colonel Gracie, who had been introduced to Andrew as a writer and amateur historian, had seen him and walked over to join him.

"Good evening, young man. Are you ready for our game of chess?" Mr. Millet asked, and Andrew replied that he was. The three men went down to the first-class smoking room, the *Titanic's* all-male domain, decorated in dark wood, green leather, and mother-of-pearl.

The fireplace was warm, and glowing coals were throwing dancing shadows on the chess pieces.

While Andrew and Mr. Millet sat over the game pieces, a man introduced to Andrew as Benjamin

Guggenheim pulled up a chair and watched the game with interest for a few minutes until someone walked over to him and spoke in a hushed tone.

"Madame Aubart is waiting for you outside in the foyer."

"If you'll excuse me, gentlemen. I'll look in on your game later." Mr. Guggenheim rose and bowed to them, then walked out of the room. Other men came by the table to chat and watch as Andrew and Mr. Millet made their moves.

John Jacob Astor, the American millionaire Andrew had read about in the newspapers, observed them with interest and went to join a group of men at a corner table. Andrew could hear their discussion of American politics as he paused with a piece before making a move.

"President Taft will be up against Woodrow Wilson for the Democratic, and Teddy Roosevelt is leading the Republicans, and that Socialist Party man, Debs, this November…"

There was other talk around the room.

"The Irish Home Rule bill is going into Parliament soon. I wonder how that will play out. We shall see in time…"

"The explorer Roald Amundsen planted a flag on the South Pole in December, just before Scott…"

"What about the Germans? They've been itching for a fight in Europe since the Franco-Prussian War."

"I have a source that tells me they've been planning for a while… surely our dreadnoughts will outwit them at sea…"

Andrew listened to the discussions until Mr. Millet cleared his throat. "Andrew, my boy, are you going to make your move?" he asked.

"I'm sorry… check," Andrew said as he placed his chess piece on a square.

"Keep your mind on the game, Mr. Elliot. This isn't the time to let your mind wander," Mr. Millet said with a slight smile. Andrew watched as Millet looked over the board thoughtfully before he made his move.

Andrew looked around the room at the other men who sat back in the green leather chairs with cigars and cigarettes, playing cards and chatting. Some were young like himself, and others had graying hair and faces lined by years of business and family concerns. He wondered if any of them ever felt the way he did at this moment, if any had ever had feelings toward another man.

Do these men ever love someone for whom the world forbids them to show affection, or do they hide it behind successful businesses, a wife and children? Will I be sitting in their place in the future?

Mr. Millet broke into his thoughts. "Shall we get some refreshments?"

"Sure, some whisky," Andrew said, and he lifted his hand to signal the steward.

He made another move to counter Mr. Millet's on the board, and then he thought about Matthew, wherever he was on the ship at that moment.

Finally, Mr. Millet made a move and called, "Checkmate. I see your mind is not on the game tonight, young man. Why not go for a walk on deck?" He folded his hands on the table.

Andrew got up, downed the whisky that had just arrived, and set the glass down. "Good night, sir. I'll see you in the morning."

Andrew got down to the third-class well deck and was heading toward the smoking room when the door opened and he saw Matthew standing in the light. They both stopped, exchanging shy smiles, and they moved closer together.

"Hello, Matthew. I guess you're wondering why I came back?" Andrew said.

"Don't tell me, you lost your cap over the rail again?" Matthew said, trying not to laugh.

Andrew shook his head. "No, I was hoping to see you again."

"But why, Andrew? You belong up there, and I belong here. We can't keep meeting like this."

"It sounds like you're trying to get rid of me, but if that's what you want…" Andrew said, turning around to walk away, but Matthew reached out and touched his sleeve.

"I was hoping I would see you again," Matthew said with a faint smile on his lips.

When Andrew heard that, he was glad it was dark so Matthew couldn't see him blushing. "You were?"

"I thought meeting you was a dream. Now I know it's real," Matthew said, his fingers still touching the sleeve of Andrew's coat. Andrew wanted to reach out to him, but he suddenly became aware of their surroundings. Every creak of a door on its hinges or sound of distant footsteps made him anxious as they both looked around.

"I know it's not a dream, because I can feel my heart beating," Andrew whispered. He reached out his hand, searching for Matthew's, then took it in his own and squeezed lightly before letting go just as someone opened a door. A man passed quickly, paying no attention to Andrew and Matthew; the stranger went through another door, leaving them alone again. A door opened once more, and this time a voice called out for Matthew.

"Hey, mate, why are you taking so long out there? We've got work to do."

"I'm sorry, Tom. I'll be right there," Matthew replied. The door shut.

"You have to go, but I'll see you again, even if I have to stand up there in first class and wait for you to appear." Andrew pointed up toward the first-class area.

"Good night, Andrew. I'll look for you, and you better be there," Matthew said, his eyes shining even in the dark.

"Good night, Matthew." Andrew remained until Matthew disappeared into the smoking room.

"Good night, Tom. I'll be down in a minute," Matthew said to his friend before Tom hurried down the stairs. Matthew pulled a packet of cigarettes from his pocket, and he was startled by the spark and hiss of a match. He saw Andrew's face in the pinpoint of light.

"What are you doing here, Andrew? I wasn't expecting you," Matthew said, trying not to sound happy to see Andrew, but he couldn't help smiling.

"I know I already said good night, and I don't care if I get in trouble…"

"You, but what about me? The other stewards may begin talking."

"I understand that, but the minutes I get to spend with you are so short that we have to take any minutes we can," Andrew said.

Matthew felt his face turn suddenly warm in the chilly air. "You wanted to see me?"

"Sure, why not?"

"I'm flattered, but I don't want to make trouble, and I'm not posh like…"

"Me? You mean having things like money and position? It might sound insane to you because we only just met, but all the money in the world doesn't buy happiness," Andrew said, snapping his fingers. Matthew looked into Andrew's face in the dim light.

"It's getting late, Andrew, and the chief or one of my mates may came looking if I'm not in my bunk, but you've given me things to think about," Matthew said, reaching out and touching Andrew's hand.

They remained together until approaching footsteps from nearby drove them their separate ways. Just before Matthew disappeared down below, Andrew stopped him.

"You can't keep me away. I'll be back, Matthew." Then Andrew was gone.

Matthew was unable to sleep, so he stared into the dark, listening to the eight other third-class stewards who shared his room snoring or shifting in their bunks. It had been two days since he thought about Lord Carson, and every revolution of the *Titanic*'s propellers carried him farther beyond Carson's reach. When they got to America, he would slip ashore with his pay and buy a one-way ticket to Texas, and Lord Carson, finding Matthew gone from the country, would turn his attentions to some other poor street boy.

Matthew allowed his mind to wander to earlier that afternoon, when Andrew Elliot came just to see him. He relived each second of the encounter, thinking over the things he should have said in the short time they'd had.

"You really shouldn't be down here. You could get us both in trouble."

"If they question me, I'll tell them that I came to thank you for recovering something I lost."

"Say thank you, tip him, and go back to where you belong, sir. That's how Captain Smith would respond."

"Then I'll say, 'Captain Smith, he's the handsomest man I've seen on board'.'"

"He'll throw you into the brig and remind you of White Star Line policy about socializing with members of the crew."

Matthew continued the conversation in his head until the throb of the engines turning over lulled him to sleep.

Chapter Eight

Friday, April twelve, 1912

Andrew had just finished breakfast and was passing through the reception room on his way back up to his room, when he saw William coming down the stairs, smiling.

"Good morning, chap. How about going for a swim after breakfast?" William said, sounding hopeful.

"I've just had breakfast, and I was going to grab a book and do some reading for a while," Andrew told him.

"I'll meet you in the reading room after I'm finished," William replied. "And then we can go down. It's all right if you don't have a bathing costume. I'm sure they have some extras or something." William winked and walked away.

Andrew went for his book, but instead of going to the reading room, he went for a walk, by habit going to the same place. He saw a number of passengers and crew down on the well deck and on the stern area, but not Matthew.

He was so lost in looking for the familiar face that he almost jumped when a voice behind him said, "Good morning, Mr. Elliot. Lovely day, isn't it?"

"Hello, Mr. Millet."

Andrew smiled, and Mr. Millet observed him in silence for a moment before he spoke, "You know, if I had some of my drawing materials handy right now, I would sketch you standing there at the rail with that look on your face. It could be the male version of *Wandering Thoughts*. I could title it *Ocean Reveries*. I could paint you as you were a moment ago, gazing out across the ocean. Perhaps your two friends could be standing next to you, engaged in conversation."

"I'm sorry, am I being that obvious, Mr. Millet?"

"Please call me, Frank, and I recognize the longing look of someone in love when I see it. There's a mixture of desire mingled with a little bit of sadness in your eyes, as if you were looking for someone far away. Am I right?"

"You're a very perceptive man, Mr. Millet… Frank."

"Do you want to talk about it?" Frank said. Andrew thought he had a kindly face, and was going to say yes, but William came walking toward them.

"There you are, Andrew. When I didn't see you in the reading room, I came looking for you, and here you are!"

"Maybe later, sir," Andrew said.

"Well, if you want to talk, a group of us will be in the smoking room this evening after dinner. Mr. Stead is going to tell us some of his ghost stories."

"Thank you. I'll take you up on that, sir," Andrew promised, and Frank Millet walked away, leaving Andrew alone with William.

"Ready for that swim now?" William asked.

Andrew was reluctant, but at the last second he said, "Sure, William, let's go."

"Excellent, just excellent," William said, rubbing his hands together.

Andrew and William found the swimming bath located on F-Deck, the lowest section of first class. A steward provided them each with a bathing costume and directed them to changing stalls alongside the pool. William took the stall beside Andrew. While Andrew was getting undressed, he could feel William's eyes on him, even through the thin walls, but William looked quickly away when he turned around. Andrew wanted to say something, but there was another man changing in the stall on the other side, so he kept his silence.

The pool was six feet of heated saltwater, and when Andrew dived in and surfaced, shaking the waterdrops out of his hair, he had to admit he enjoyed the plunge. A second later, William came up next to him, and he could feel William's leg touch his. Andrew's response was to swim away to the end of the pool, doing a couple of quick laps before he joined William, who was treading water along one side.

"The attendant isn't looking, Andrew," William said, glancing around the room. They were alone. He reached to grab at Andrew, but just then a door swung open, and the pool attendant returned. Andrew was relieved. William slapped the water with one hand. A foot or two away, Andrew looked at him.

"No thanks, William. Not now or ever. I'm engaged, as you and everyone else point out to me," Andrew said, swimming quickly away and doing two more laps before paddling over to where William still clung to the side of the pool.

"I'm already tired of this. Let's go," William said, swimming toward the ladder at the end.

Andrew remained where he was, treading water until he plunged below the surface. When he came up again, he did two more laps back and forth, and then he joined William, who was leaning on the wall watching him. Andrew walked by him, grabbed a towel from a table, took a shower to rinse away the saltwater, and padded across the tiles to the dressing room. William joined him a few minutes later. He was scowling, and his thin lips were so tight together they made a narrow, straight line. Andrew backed away, because it seemed as if William would strike him at any second.

"What's wrong, William? You look angry about something."

"Nothing!" William snapped. Andrew shrugged and finished drying off, then got dressed. He was waiting outside the door to the swimming bath while William finished dressing, and then he came out to join him.

"Claire's waiting for us. I think she might want to play cards again," William grumbled, then resumed walking.

Andrew remained on the step, looking up, as William disappeared around the corner, his footsteps fading. He saw a door on his right that read Crew Only. He tried the knob, and it opened. Cautiously he stepped through it. Looking to his right and left, he found himself in a long corridor. He marked where he came from and started exploring.

He passed closed doors on both sides of the corridor—storerooms, pantries, and crewmen's quarters. Andrew heard activity and voices from behind some of the rooms he passed, but he couldn't hear what was being said, and then he walked by a half-open door and stopped.

Andrew saw the familiar profile standing with his back to him, looking into a small mirror, straightening his jacket and tie. Andrew didn't think Matthew noticed him until Matthew gasped and turned around quickly.

"Andrew, what are you doing here?" Matthew said with a smile, moving toward Andrew's outstretched arms, but footsteps outside in the hall stopped him. A stewardess passed by with a cart of laundry, and she was gone before Andrew spoke, "I had to see you again, Matthew. I haven't been able to think about anything else." He moved closer to Matthew and kissed him. The kiss lasted only a second, but they were both breathless when it was over.

Matthew looked at the clock over the door and then down at Andrew. "I'm glad you came to find me, but you ought not to be here. If you're caught, we could both get into trouble."

"You said that before, but what can they do? Fire you and ban me from traveling on the *Titanic* for a year or two?"

"They could clap us both into prison. Our feelings are against the law."

"Damn the law and damn prison. I can kiss you again if I want to. I really like you, Matthew, more than you can imagine, and if that weren't the case, I wouldn't be risking trouble if I didn't feel anything," Andrew said, his tone impatient.

"How can you be sure? It's only been two days."

"Meeting you that night was the best thing that's happened to me on this voyage, Matthew. Otherwise, I would have gotten off the *Titanic* in Queenstown." Andrew saw Matthew back up, glancing quickly toward the door. "What's wrong?"

"Nothing, but I'm on duty shortly. They may come looking for me," Matthew said.

"I'm not going away until you tell me what you're feeling," Andrew said, standing close to Matthew, waiting. He watched Matthew fingering a silver badge on his jacket, and then he shut the door.

"Yes, I like you too, Andrew. It's true, I only wish we could have more time together than these short meetings… I guess I'll have to be happy until we reach

New York," Matthew said. Andrew saw Matthew's body shiver slightly, and then he took Andrew in his arms and kissed him. The kiss was longer than the previous brief peck on the lips; it was warm and lingering. Andrew felt as if everything else ceased to exist—it was only him in Matthew's arms, holding him with surprising power.

They stopped when they heard a sound outside, looking at each other until they could breathe again. There were footsteps outside the door, coming closer, and both of them were sweating when the steps finally died away. Andrew went to the door and opened it partway to look out.

"Okay, I'll go for now, but I am going to see you again. My cabin number is A-17 if you get away." Andrew was disappointed that he couldn't stay, but he turned, then paused in the door to exchange a final look with Matthew before he left.

Matthew remained standing motionless in the center of the room for a few minutes. He could still feel the electricity of their kiss on his lips when he finally moved. Andrew cared about him, and it didn't matter that he was a third-class steward who served ale to working-class men. No, Andrew had taken the chance to sneak down from above and see him. Matthew was flattered that such a handsome young man would take the time to even consider him.

Would Lord Carson have done the same thing for me if we met on this voyage? Will Andrew disappear at the end of the trip, moving on to some other young man?

Negative thoughts coming so soon after such happiness sobered him quickly. He would have to believe Andrew was an honorable man, and he prayed he was correct.

As he left the cabin, closing the door behind him, he ran into Tom coming down the hall.

"Come on, mate. It's nearly time for us to open up the smoking room, and we'll be late." Tom paused as Matthew was touching his finger to his lips. "You haven't gone daft, have you?"

"No, why did you say that?" Matthew asked, pulling his hand away from his face.

"You were rubbing your face like there was something there."

"Sorry. Come on, let's go before we're late and the passengers pound down the doors." Matthew walked away, leaving Tom to catch up. Tom stepped up next to him just before they reached the third-class smoking room.

"Is this about the young man from first class?" Tom asked.

"Certainly not. Why would you ask that?" Matthew said quickly. "Believe it or not, lad, I'm on your side, but I don't want you to get into trouble."

"Thanks, Tom but I can handle myself."

"I'm not saying you can't, but wait until you're in a discreet place on shore—"

"You won't say anything, will you?" Matthew interrupted Tom.

"As one friend who shares your feeling to another, your secret's safe with me."

Andrew sat reading in *a wicker chair in the Café Parisian*, still feeling the static of Matthew's kiss on his lips. He had never been kissed like that. Not even Robert had kissed him with such tenderness and passion.

Robert, whose letter still remained unfinished in the pages of his book. *I'll finish it sometime, maybe in New York*, Andrew thought. He removed the paper, and after tearing it in half once and then twice, he dropped it in a wastebasket in a corner. *Maybe I'll write another letter sometime, perhaps when we reach New York.*

He returned to his book and sat reading, idly listening to the throb of the engines and the conversations going on around him, ***the clink of cup and saucer***, ***the roar of the ocean rolling past the window***. He tried to get back into his book, but after half an hour, he had read the same paragraph over and over again, so he closed the book, got up, and went ***up on deck*** for a walk.

Andrew went out on the open end of the first-class promenade overlooking the bow and faced into the wind, letting it whip his hair and face. There was a hint of ocean spray touching his lips.

Never in his life had he done as much thinking as he had on this voyage. He wished Matthew was standing up here with him to share in the joy he was feeling, to experience the power of *Titanic* as she plowed forward through the waves. Andrew felt free.

There was no Claire clinging to him and talking about a marriage he didn't want, and no William with his hungry, greedy eyes watching him. Even Robert's face became a distant thought as wispy as the waterdrops that touched his face. Andrew only had a tiny pang of regret that he hadn't left the ship in Queenstown. He'd heard from his bedroom steward that one of the engine room crew had hidden among the shore- bound mailbags. Andrew laughed, picturing himself hiding among them, but then he would have missed ***meeting*** Matthew.

He knew so little about Matthew, and their only chances to talk had been so fleeting.

Heavy footsteps sounded on the deck behind him, and then Claire's voice shattered his cheerful thoughts.

"There you are, Andrew. We've been looking for you everywhere," she said, grabbing his arm.

William licked his lips and said, "We were looking for you to join us for a walk and a game of cards before luncheon. How about it?"

"I'm not in the mood for cards, but the walk would be fine," Andrew said, taking a few steps ahead of them before Claire again took his arm. William fell in step beside them, hemming Andrew in.

The spell of freedom was broken.

They strolled along, stopping to chat with the other ladies and gentlemen they passed along the way.

Andrew paused when he saw Thomas Andrews with a pad of paper and a pencil, standing at the rail, leaning over the side, and making notes. Mr. Andrews smiled when Andrew came up next to him, followed by Claire and her brother.

"Mr. Andrews, are you still working on this wonderful ship of yours?"

"Always, Mr. Elliot. I designed her to be perfect in every way, but there's always room for improvements," Mr. Andrews said.

Over his shoulder, Andrew could see Claire and William were anxious to keep moving. Thomas Andrews was busy making some notes, so Andrew said, "Excuse us, Mr. Andrews." He smiled and walked away, with Claire taking his arm.

Farther down the deck, a woman dressed in a coat of blue velvet and cream-colored lace, walking with two other women, looked at Claire and her brother and turned to whisper to her companions. Andrew remembered her from the dining room. *Claire gave her a half-smile, nodding as she passed.*

"I've always wanted to see the pyramids and the sphinx," Andrew said. William was silent, and Claire almost let out a laugh.

"They're overrated and crowded with tourists."

"Well, I should like to see them anyway," Andrew said. *I thought you and William have never been?*

"Maybe next winter," Claire said sharply, obviously not wishing to pursue the subject.

"Come on, you two lovebirds, let's enjoy our walk. It's such a beautiful, sunny day," William said.

Andrew walked along with them and only half listened to their conversation. He wanted to get away.

They paused on the boat deck, looking out to sea. Andrew thought it was the most beautiful sight he had ever seen, and the sunlight on the waves reminded him of the loch just beyond the manor house in the Highlands. A slight pang of homesickness overcame him, and he wanted to be back home riding his horse among the heather and stopping by the small cliff overlooking the water near the house, with a view of castle ruins on an island in the middle of the loch. It was so peaceful and beautiful, even in a storm.

"Andrew Elliot, what are you thinking about? Were you even listening to me?" Claire asked.

"I was thinking about home," Andrew replied simply, not wishing to elaborate.

Claire clucked her tongue and turned her head away. She muttered something, but Andrew didn't hear what it was.

Matthew leaned over a table, going over the polished surface with a towel. Next to him was a tray of empty glasses. The smoking room was already crowded at three o'clock with the usual groups of men playing cards and checkers. The air was heavy with the smoke of foreign blends of cigars and cigarettes, and with languages Matthew had never heard before.

"What's the matter with you, boy? You've been walking around in a daze all morning, and you've been wiping down that table for two minutes," Tom said.

"Nothing's wrong, Tom. I was just thinking about something, that's all."

"You know you can talk to me if you want, but right now get your head out of the clouds. We have work to do," Tom said, smiling and gesturing around the room.

The door opened, and an officer in a dark blue uniform entered. Matthew and Tom tried to look busy as he approached. The officer walked up to Tom.

"The captain and purser wish to speak to you, if you can spare a few minutes," the officer said. Matthew and Tom exchanged glances.

"I haven't done anything wrong," Tom said.

"Not that I know of. Just come along," the officer said, motioning for Tom to follow.

When Tom returned to duty twenty minutes later, he was frowning. Matthew asked him what had happened, but Tom didn't respond, and the rest of the morning and afternoon he avoided Matthew.

Chapter Nine

Andrew's mind was not on the card game that he reluctantly agreed to join, after all. He kept glancing at his pocket watch, trying to come up with an excuse to leave and go to the usual place overlooking the well deck to third-class. It would have been easy to drop the cards, stand up, and leave, but William would have insisted on walking with him, or Claire would have pouted loudly. His chance came when the bugler sounded that it was time to dress for dinner.

Cards were set down, promises to meet again after dinner were exchanged, and Andrew left the lounge, keeping himself ahead of them. Instead of returning to his cabin, he went in the other direction, toward the stern, to the end of the first-class promenade.

Looking over the rail, he saw that the deck was empty, but then he saw a familiar brown-haired man in a white jacket come out through a door. Andrew climbed the rail, down the ladder, and was standing in front of him before Matthew could disappear down the ladder to his quarters.

They smiled when they saw each other.

"Hello, Matthew. I had to see you."

Matthew wished he could rush into Andrew's arms. "I'm glad you came. I was afraid I would not see you."

"Are you still on duty?" Andrew said.

"I'm on duty until midnight, and then it starts all over again tomorrow morning," Matthew said.

"What's wrong?" Andrew asked, frowning.

"Nothing at all, just tired." Matthew smiled, trying to hide his worry at Tom's odd behavior.

"I know I already told you *what cabin in in, but* I just wanted to make sure you remember. We don't have to do anything. We can talk at least," Andrew said, sounding hopeful that Matthew would come.

Matthew hesitated, torn between wanting to say yes and refusing because he didn't want to get in trouble. "I can't promise you I'll come, but if I can get away, I'll try," Matthew said.

Matthew was glad for the brief visit, and after Andrew left, he stood alone staring over the rail.

Footsteps behind him made Matthew turn, and he saw Tom coming toward him with an officer and a sailor.

"Matthew Ahearn, the captain would like to speak with you," the officer said.

Matthew felt his body go numb, and he wished Andrew was there with him. "What have I done?" he asked, following the officer.

"I don't know. I have my orders. He wants to speak with you and sent me to fetch you along," the officer said.

Matthew looked back over his shoulder, but Tom had gone inside.

As he was escorted to the bridge, Matthew glanced around nervously. He had never met Captain E.J. Smith before; the man looked like a typical sea captain to Matthew—gray hair and beard, light eyes, and weathered hands. Captain Smith motioned for Matthew to follow him into a small room off the wheelhouse, filled with navigational charts and blueprints. The purser, Hugh McElroy, and the chief third-class steward, Matthew's boss, James Kieran, were also there.

The captain closed the door, and there were a few moments of silence in the room while Matthew stood facing the three men. The captain reached into a pocket and pulled out two slips of paper, which he handed to Matthew.

Matthew glanced at them; they were both wireless messages. One was a weather report warning of ice far ahead in their path—and the captain took that one back quickly. It was the second one Matthew was supposed to see.

Chief Inspect Winters, Scotland Yard to Captain Smith, Titanic Steward Matthew Ahearn wanted for questioning.

Retain and return on next voyage.

"Can you explain this, Mr. Ahearn?" the captain asked.

"I don't know what it's about, sir. I haven't done anything," Matthew said right away, thinking that Lord Carson must be behind this.

"We've discussed this and decided that you are suspended from your duties, and you'll be confined to an empty cabin until we return to Southampton on the next voyage. Your pay will be forfeited in recompense for the price of a ticket." Captain Smith's voice sounded like a death sentence in Matthew's ears.

Matthew lifted his head to speak. "Won't I even be allowed a walk on deck?"

"That can be arranged," one of the officers said. Matthew felt his legs turn to rubber, and he wanted to say more, but his mind wouldn't let him form the words he wanted.

The purser sat back in his chair and asked, "Do you have anything to say, Mr. Ahearn?"

"No, sir. I can't explain this," Matthew said, his voice coming out as a croak.

"Very well, I'll have a sailor escort you to the room," the chief steward said as he reached into his pocket and removed a set of keys. The captain and purser went out, and Captain Smith returned with a sailor who would take Matthew to the waiting prison.

Andrew was silent during dinner despite the efforts of William and Claire, who steered him away from his usual place with Frank Millet, Colonel Butt, and Mr. Stead.

"Where did you wander off to, Andrew? We were worried you might have fallen overboard," Claire said, batting her eyelashes.

Andrew flushed and looked down at the veal and potatoes in front of him. "I needed to go for a walk on the boat deck before I went to get dressed," Andrew informed her, finally taking a bite of his food before it got cold.

"You've been quite attracted to a particular spot *out* on deck for some reason, chap, but I can't see the fascination for a lot of steerage passengers and whatnot."

"No reason. It just seems like a decent space where there's not a lot of people about," Andrew said flatly, and that seemed to satisfy the pair. The rest of the meal continued without much conversation, for which Andrew was grateful.

Andrew gulped down a cup of coffee after dinner and left the dining room before William or Claire could stop him. He went up to the boat deck and leaned against the railing. He lifted his head into the wind— which tousled his hair—and looked up at the stars in the night sky and then down at the ocean tossing in endless waves from the *Titanic*'s side.

Making up his mind to see Matthew again, Andrew headed down toward the third-class smoking room.

When he entered, he found the room crowded and saw three stewards moving among the passengers. He waited off to one side, staring every time the door opened, but each time it was someone other than Matthew.

Is Matthew not on duty tonight and he didn't tell me?

Andrew saw a crewman nearby finishing with a group of men smoking and laughing, and Andrew called him over. The steward looked at him curiously, obviously taking in his expensive clothing.

"Is there anything I can do for you, sir?" the steward asked.

"Yes, I'm looking for one of your crew members, Matthew Ahearn."

"Oh, I think he's off duty tonight, but then I haven't seen him all day."

"Maybe someone else knows," Andrew said.

The steward nodded and stopped another steward who was passing by.

"John, do you know where Ahearn is?"

"How should I know? I don't keep track of everybody around here," John replied curtly and went on his way.

"It's most likely he's either off duty or he's having his dinner. I really must go, sir. Duty calls." The steward smiled and went to a nearby table.

Andrew leaned back against the wall. He was cheered by the thought that maybe Matthew was either having a late dinner or already asleep.

"I'll see him tomorrow morning," Andrew said, walking out of the room.

Andrew entered the first-class smoking room and found Colonel Butt sitting at a table with a cigar and a glass of whisky. He already knew Mr. Millet and William Stead, but there was another gentleman seated with them to whom Colonel Butt introduced him.

"Welcome, Andrew. You already know everyone, so have a seat," Colonel Butt said, standing up and pulling over one of the green leather chairs for Andrew. Andrew shook hands with Mr. Gracie. A steward brought Andrew a glass of whisky, and he sat back and listened to the end of the conversation he had come in on.

"... I have a copy of my newly published work, *The Truth about Chickamauga,* on board with me. I loaned it to Mr. Straus, so I'll see that he gives it to you when he's through looking it over," Mr. Gracie said to Colonel Butt. Then Mr. Gracie turned toward William Stead.

Mr. Millet leaned over and whispered into Andrew's ear. "We will have our little talk in a while, young man," he said, and then he turned to William Stead. "Why don't you tell us one of your ghost stories?"

Mr. Stead sat back in his chair, looking around the little group, his eyes stopping on Andrew, almost as if he could see deep into his soul.

Andrew took a sip of whisky to warm the sudden chill he felt. He looked across the table at Mr. Stead, at his piercing dark eyes and gray beard. He reminded Andrew of an Old Testament prophet.

Mr. Stead stared over their heads as if fixing on a point in the room, and then he pulled out a pocket watch and said to the men gathered with him, "I wanted to make note of the time. It's Friday the twelfth of April, and when I finish this story, it shall be the thirteenth, for the superstitious among you. Now as you know, I've spent some time in Egypt, and while I was there, I became familiar with a man named Douglas Murray, who was among a group who discovered the tomb of a priestess of Amun-Ra..." Stead rested his hands over his stomach.

Andrew and the other men leaned forward in their chairs to listen.

"When Mr. Murray and his team of archeologists discovered the sealed tomb of the priestess under the floor of the temple, the hieroglyphics etched into the stone warned them of a curse on everyone who should disturb her resting place. Well, of course, in the name of science and history, they broke the seal." Mr. Stead paused, and Andrew noticed that the room was strangely silent except for the faint rumble of the engines. He wondered if anyone else noticed it as well.

"When they removed the lid of the sarcophagus, they were the first men to glimpse the tortured face of the priestess in three thousand seven hundred years. They brought the mummy with them to London, and one of the members of the team died on the voyage, another went mad and ended up in an asylum, and similar fates struck all the members of the expedition.

Even Mr. Murray didn't escape the curse, going bankrupt and having to sell his collection of artifacts to an American museum—the mummy of the priestess as well."

It was at that second that the clock on the fireplace mantel struck midnight. Andrew almost jumped at the sound of the chime.

"Well, gentlemen, it's now Saturday, April thirteenth. I bid you good night, since the stewards are anxious to close down the room for the night." William Stead stood up and led the men from the room; only Andrew and Mr. Millet remained behind.

Andrew liked hearing Mr. Stead's ghost story; it made him think of his family home in Edinburgh, which possessed two ghosts of its own. One was the spirit of a relative who had passed away in 1780—a great-great aunt whose portrait graced the main staircase landing; her spirit remained stationed in an upstairs hallway window, weeping for her husband, *who had been lost at sea*. Many guests complained of being wakened in the middle of the night by someone outside their rooms who sounded as if she were in great distress, and there were some people who smelled lavender, which was said to have been her favorite scent. The other ghost was a soldier ancestor who passed away in the house after he had been shot in a duel. Andrew was used to hearing him walk the halls at night, and to Andrew the ghosts were harmless, a part of the old house's charm and character.

Claire and William had said they heard the noises but dismissed them as the wind or the age of the house. Andrew was still thinking about it all when Mr. Millet reminded him of his presence with a gentle touch on the shoulder.

"Come on, my boy. We will go for a walk, and you can tell me what's on your mind," Mr. Millet said as they stepped outside.

The promenade was deserted except for them, and they walked in silence for a moment before Andrew spoke. He wasn't sure how much he should open up to this kind older man, but he had to talk to someone.

"I don't really know where to begin, but did you ever love someone who others consider beneath you?"

"Others, meaning who?"

"My father didn't believe my relationship was appropriate for a son of the house of Elliot. He sent me away to avoid a scandal, and now…"

"Tell me something, my boy. Was it a young lady or a man? I won't be shocked if you tell me, and your secret is safe between us," Mr. Millet finished speaking, and for a minute there was only the sound of the ocean and someone plinking out a popular song on the keys of a piano. The sound came from nearby, on the upper landing of the grand staircase.

Andrew didn't know what to say, but he swallowed hard and blurted out, "I *think* I'm falling in love *he's a* steward from steerage, sir," he felt relieved to have told someone.

Mr. Millet looked down at the teak deck at their feet and then up at Andrew, who was relieved. Mr. Millet looked thoughtful, and then asked, "Does *he* feel the same way about you?"

"Maybe. We don't get any real chances to talk. This whole ship is a maze of barriers erected to keep us apart."

"And never the twain shall meet. Plus, he could lose his job if you were caught."

"That pretty much sums it up, sir," Andrew said.

Mr. Millet slowed his steps and walked over to the railing to look out over the ocean racing past below. Andrew joined him.

"If you want to be with your young man, then I would caution you to wait until we reach New York, my boy. Be mindful of his position on the ship, as well as your own. If, however, love won't wait, and it never does, then I would ask you to be discreet for both your sakes, *a ship is a small town, and gossip gets about*," Mr. Millet said.

"Thank you for your honesty, sir. I'll keep what you said in mind," Andrew said with a faint smile.

"I think it's time we both retired for the night. You have some things to think about… Good night." Mr. Millet nodded and walked away, leaving Andrew at the rail.

Chapter Ten

Saturday, April thirteen, 1912

"Stop eating so fast, Andrew, or you'll end up with indigestion," William said from across the dining table, watching Andrew eat breakfast. Claire sniffed. "You've been acting very strange lately. Last night you ate dinner and hurried away, leaving us without a fourth for cards, and now you're doing the exact same thing. I hope this isn't a preview of our married life. *Sitting at the table, rushing through meals,* and hiding behind the newspaper like every other man in the world."

"I've been busy," Andrew said, not caring to go into detail with

Claire. He did notice, however, that they both frowned at the same time. "Not reading and writing, I hope?" Claire said.

"I was in the smoking room last night, listening to one of Mr. Stead's ghost stories. Very fascinating stuff. I'll have to look for his writings," Andrew said.

Claire and William laughed.

"You don't believe in that nonsense, do you?" Claire said. "The Douglas's told us your home in Edinburgh was haunted. Sure, we heard the wind howling and some creaks while we were staying there, but we didn't experience rattling chains or moans in the night."

I thought you didn't believe in those things, Andrew thought. "Let's change the subject, shall we, Claire? This has been a wonderful voyage so far, so let's not spoil it with arguments," Andrew said calmly. He was secretly pleased to notice that both Claire and William were reduced to silence, and when they finally did talk, it was to plan another card game and find two more partners.

He left them after breakfast to write a letter to his mother back home.

On board RMS Titanic Dear Mother,

I promised I would write, and I hope your receipt of this letter from New York will put to rest any fear you had about traveling on the Titanic. She's a beautiful ship, like spending a week in a palace by the seashore and looking over the side of the ship is like standing on the edge of a cliff. I'll write more tomorrow.

Love, Andrew

Andrew thought about sending one to Robert, but as the distance between them grew ever wider, the memory, however pleasant it may have been, began to fade. It was his encounter with Robert that had flung him into an engagement with a woman he didn't love and a supposed friendship with her lecherous brother. Andrew did start another letter to Robert, but he only got as far as the date before he tore it up and threw away the pieces.

He posted his finished letters in a box in the lounge, and then went for a walk. He went to his usual spot looking over the stern well deck. There were several steerage passengers about playing games and standing at the rails looking out over the ocean. He saw crewmen among them, but he didn't spot a familiar white steward's jacket.

Matthew sat on the edge of a bunk and stared at the tiled floor at his feet. It was obvious the police had traced him to Southampton and from there to the *Titanic*. That had to be why he was being sent back to England. He looked up at a soft knock on the door and the click of a key in the lock. A crewman let Tom in and closed the door, leaving them alone. Tom came and sat next to Matthew.

"What is this, mate? What is it you're supposed to have done?"

"It doesn't make any difference, Tom, I'll be hanged... I would rather not talk about it," Matthew said, almost on the verge of tears.

Tom reached out and put an arm around him. "If you need a character, you can count on me." Tom tried to smile.

"Thanks, Tom." Matthew tried to sound cheerful. He looked at his fingers and then back at his friend.

They were both silent for a few minutes, and finally Tom said, "Is there anything I can do, Matthew?"

Matthew hesitated, looking down at his twined fingers. "Can you get a message to someone?"

Nobody noticed Andrew when he walked into the third-class smoking room and looked around for Matthew. There was a steward he didn't recognize and another who came out of a side door. The second steward stared at Andrew for a moment, then came over to him.

"Can I help you with something, sir?" the steward asked politely. Andrew recognized him as the steward who was also on duty *whenever* he came to see Matthew.

Andrew stalled for a moment. "I was looking for someone, but I don't see him. Perhaps I…"

The steward leaned in closer and said to him, "Are you Andrew Elliot?"

"Yes. Is Matthew around?"

"Might I have a word with you in private?" the steward said, motioning Andrew toward the pantry. Andrew followed him inside.

"What is this? What's happened to Matthew?" Andrew asked.

"Matthew is confined to quarters and will be returned to England on the next voyage," the steward said.

The words fell on Andrew's ears like the heavy blows of a hammer. "What? What has he done?"

"That's just it, Mr. Elliot. I have asked him, and he won't tell me."

"Can I see him?" *Andrew asked, trying not to sound anxious about hearing the news.*

"You would have to ask permission of Captain Smith, sir," the man informed him.

Andrew stood there for a moment in shock. The steward took a bottle of whisky from a cupboard and poured a small glass for Andrew. He took it and swallowed, then set the glass back down.

"Thank you for telling me... Mr...?" Andrew said with a trace of a smile.

"It's Tom, sir. He's a good lad, and I don't believe he would do anything wrong. There must be a mistake."

"I better go see the captain now. Thank you again, Tom."

Andrew was anxious as he passed through the gate that separated the *Titanic*'s bridge and wheelhouse from the passengers' promenade. He saw Captain Smith standing outside looking forward. The captain didn't see Andrew at first.

What if he doesn't want to talk to me? Andrew thought as he stepped forward.

An officer walked around him and addressed the captain. Andrew couldn't hear their conversation, but Captain Smith looked directly at him. He seemed like a kindly man, but Andrew could feel his palms sweating as the captain beckoned him to his side.

"Good day. You're Mr. Elliot, aren't you?" Captain Smith said.

"Yes, sir. It's a fine day, and the *Titanic* is beautiful and so powerful," Andrew said, trying to get to the point of his visit.

"Below our feet, the turbines are generating sixteen thousand horsepower, and sometime during the voyage, we'll light the last four boilers," Captain Smith said, facing out over the bow again. Andrew stood next to him, watching the waves toss left and right. He and the captain were silent, side by side, until Smith cleared his throat and said, "I don't think you came up here to discuss the technical workings of the *Titanic*. What can I do for you?"

"I was wondering if I could have a word with you about something, captain."

"Go ahead, young man."

"This concerns a member of your crew, a steward, Matthew Ahearn," Andrew said, relieved to have spoken at last.

"I really can't discuss ship's business with passengers, Mr. Elliot, but may I ask—why does the welfare of one of my people concern you?" Andrew turned away, looking down at the deck at his feet and then back up at the captain. "I would like to see him, if I may, sir," Andrew said.

The captain studied Andrew's face in silence, and it felt to Andrew like he was going to refuse him, but then Captain Smith nodded and said, "May I ask why?"

"Well, I have spoken with Mr. Ahearn, and I'm concerned for him. That's all," Andrew said, his hand brushing the wood of the rail in front of him.

Captain Smith nodded again. "Well, I don't think there's any harm in your going to visit him."

"Thank you for understanding, captain," Andrew said, smiling faintly.

Captain Smith went to a desk and pulled out a sheet of paper. He dipped a fountain pen into an inkwell and began to write something. He finished and handed the paper to Andrew.

"Give this to any third-class steward, and they'll take you to see Mr. Ahearn."

"Thank you, Captain Smith. I appreciate this more than you know."

Andrew followed a steward down a flight of stairs, through an open gate from second class, and around a corner at the end of a short passage. The crewman put a key in the lock and opened the door.

Andrew and Matthew stood face to face, and Andrew noticed Matthew's eyes were red. The steward backed out of the room.

"I'll wait in the hall. You have ten minutes," he said and closed the door behind him.

Alone at last, they were both silent for a moment. Andrew looked about the room. There was one small porthole, four bunks, a table between them, and a washstand with towels and a couple of drinking glasses. He noticed the exposed pipes and plain white walls.

"Your friend Tom told me you were here, and I went right to the captain," Andrew said, motioning for Matthew to sit down. They sat next to each other on the bunk, their hands touching.

"I'm happy you came, Andrew. I'm only sorry you have to see me like this," Matthew said, wiping his eyes.

"Do you know what this is about?" Andrew asked.

Matthew nodded, and Andrew closed his hand over Matthew's. "I can hardly believe you're here, but this is impossible, Andrew, and you know it is."

"Why? I can talk to whomever I want," Andrew said.

"Thank you for coming to see me. It means a lot to me," Matthew whispered.

Andrew leaned close to him and wrapped an arm around his shoulder. He handed Matthew his handkerchief to wipe his eyes.

"I care about you, Matthew, and I'll think of a way to help you out of this. In the meantime, don't worry," Andrew said.

"That's easy for you to say, don't worry, sitting over there, isn't it?" Matthew sighed.

"I'm serious, Matthew. I'll think of a way to help you through this." Andrew held Matthew's hand in his own, squeezing lightly.

"I've waited for someone to say that and mean it, but there are things you need to know about me, Andrew, things that might shock you," Matthew almost choked on the words, looking down at the table, his fingers pinching the fabric of the woolen blanket on the bunk.

"What could you have done that could be so bad?"

"I don't know where to begin."

"Start at the beginning. That's always the best place."

"He was so decent to me at first. He stood up for me when that shopkeeper wanted to throw me in prison over a loaf of bread. He was gone when I woke up in that hotel, and when I left, he was lying at the bottom of the stairs. I got scared, so I ran. The police questioned the rector of the church. He gave me the money to reach Southampton."

Matthew was talking so fast that Andrew couldn't understand most of what he was saying. Andrew reached into his pocket and pulled out a silver flask with a crest on it. He stood up, poured a bit of the contents into one of the glasses, and gave it to Matthew.

"Here, drink this, and calm down. Who saved you from arrest and then was found at the bottom of a stairway?"

"Lord Carson." Matthew looked as if he was about to cry.

Andrew handed him a handkerchief and stayed in thoughtful silence before he asked, "Where were you before you found him lying there?" Andrew felt as if he sounded like Sherlock Holmes, but he had to get the information, even if they were a thousand miles from England.

"We both had some whisky, and I fell asleep, and when I woke up, he was gone. Left me with nothing but a one-pound note. I was leaving when I saw him there.

He was bleeding and had a bump on his head," Matthew said, taking a gulp of whisky.

Andrew thought about that for a minute. It was obvious that Matthew and Lord Carson had been together, but it wasn't the time for jealousy, so he wasn't going to ask about that. "So, you got scared and ran?" Matthew nodded.

"I would have done the same thing. Did you check to see if he was still breathing?" Andrew asked, noticing that Matthew had calmed down a little.

"He was. He opened his eyes and saw me, and I heard him whisper my name," Matthew said with a sigh. "They're sending me back to England, and I'm confined down here until the *Titanic*'s return voyage."

"I'm sorry, truly, Matthew."

"All because of a bloody loaf of bread. Go away, Andrew. Find someone else and don't bother with me. Aren't there any toffs up there in first class?" Matthew snapped.

"I suppose there are, but I'm not..." Andrew stopped himself before he said *I'm not beginning to fall in love with any of them*. It was only natural that a man would blow off steam in a situation like this. He gripped Matthew's hand. "Go ahead—be angry if it'll help. I'm not going to let you face this alone."

Matthew's frown softened, and he whispered, "Thanks, Andrew."

"That's better. You have a handsome smile—" Andrew was interrupted by a knock, but he managed to kiss Matthew before the door swung open.

The steward appeared, and Andrew got up.

"Do they let you out of this room at all?" Andrew paused to ask Matthew.

"I can walk on the third-class promenade on the stern probably in the morning and after tea. I don't know…"

"I'll be there," Andrew said before the door separated them.

Chapter Eleven

Andrew returned to first class, and in his cabin, he found a note from Claire left by his steward. It was only three words, but they felt like a chain tying him to Claire and her brother.

Cards after Dinner.

Andrew crumpled the note and stuffed it in his pocket. He would tell them *No, I won't join your game* when he spoke to them at dinner.

There was a soft knock on his door, and Claire called to him. "Andrew…"

Andrew sighed and opened the door. He stepped into the hall and shut the door behind him.

"Even in 1912, a woman isn't allowed to enter a man's room," Claire huffed.

"Those are the rules, unless we're married, or you are an older female relative. Why are you here, Claire? Dinner won't be announced for a couple of hours yet," Andrew said.

"William is down at the swimming bath, and I thought this would be a perfect opportunity for us to take a stroll and talk."

Claire reached out and took Andrew's arm, and they walked across the lobby in front of the grand staircase, through the vestibule, and out onto the promenade deck. The sun was beginning to lower in the sky, and Andrew marveled at the brilliant colors of yellow, red, gold, and blue. Claire led him away from the rail, and she spoke first.

"I didn't bring you out to look at the sunset. I wanted to talk about our wedding. I have a list down in the cabin of things that need to be done."

"What's there to discuss? You and my father seem to have it all under control. It's my duty to show up at the church on the wedding day," Andrew said, hoping he didn't sound sarcastic. If he did, Claire took no notice of it.

"I was thinking about where we shall live. I don't desire staying in your parents' home with a ghost. I would prefer our own place, maybe London," Claire said.

"A place like my aunt and uncle's?"

"Yes. They mentioned it one night at dinner. They only stay there for three or four months. The rest of the year the house lies idle and inviting."

"What's your point exactly, Claire? We can get our own house in London or Edinburgh. It doesn't matter where we live," Andrew said.

"Well, I was thinking maybe they'll let us live in the house the rest of the time, and we can go to Edinburgh when they need it," Claire said.

"That home belongs to my uncle and aunt. I'm not going to put them out of it," Andrew snapped.

Claire huffed, and looked to Andrew to say something else.

He was silent. *Have such living arrangements already been made between my father and this woman?*

They had reached the end of the first-class section, and Andrew walked over and stood at the rail. Looking down at the stern well deck, he wished that any second Matthew would appear. Near the entrance, four young men were playing an impromptu game, kicking a ball to one another. Boisterous laughter and the applause of their small audience reached up to the first-class deck.

"Who are you looking for, Andrew?" Claire asked, moving close to him.

"I was just standing here watching the game. Maybe I'll go down and join them," Andrew answered.

"With them? They're not our kind of *people*." Claire shuddered. She backed away from the rail and pulled at Andrew's sleeve. They walked on for a few minutes, and Andrew became aware that Claire looked as if she was about to say something. He was correct.

"You seem to have taken quite an interest in steerage lately, Andrew Elliot. I don't think your father would be pleased. I know I'm not."

"What do you mean?" Andrew asked.

"You've been seen coming and going down to the third-class decks," Claire said in an accusing voice.

Andrew kept his face impassive. "Out with it, Claire. We dock on Wednesday. So, what if I do go down to third-class? It's none of your business where I go."

"I think your father would like to know."

"He's back in Edinburgh, and we're here on the *Titanic*," Andrew said.

Claire laughed, then reached into her pocket and pulled out a piece of paper. Andrew recognized it as the form wireless messages are written on. He tried not to let her see the startled look on his face.

"Go down there again, and I send this." Claire thrust the paper into his hand. He looked at it.

Andrew has been seen with *someone* in steerage. Please advise.

Andrew wadded it up and threw it over the side.

"It doesn't matter. I can write another one, unless you give me a reason not to. Stay away from your friend down there. Do you understand me?"

"Stop pretending that you're so shocked. I wonder what my parents would say if I was to tell them some things all about you and your brother... about Egypt and some other rumors that have reached me. About Sir Cliverford and the true state of your affairs. *That you're both nothing but fortune hunters.*"

"From whom? The gossips? That's all they are—tales spun by tattletales."

"Maybe they are, but I think my father would like to know about them before the wedding band is on your finger. I've been investigating all the stories I've heard," Andrew said with a trace of a smile. He looked sideways at Claire, and she looked away from him, out to the ocean, slowly she backed away. Andrew took a few steps, then stopped, forcing her to halt also and return to where he was standing.

"You think I'm not going to send that wire to your parents? Let me catch you in third-class again," Claire said. Andrew laughed, and Claire snapped at him, "Stop laughing this instant!"

"I'll do whatever I please, and if you object to that, then I'll send a wire to my parents telling them that you and your brother are a couple of pretenders to wealth and that I'm calling off the wedding. I'm not afraid of you or your brother, Claire," Andrew said, facing her. He could tell Claire was building up to respond, but the door leading from the grand staircase opened. William came out smiling and walked toward them.

"It's beautiful to see you two lovebirds together for once."

"We were taking a walk. Would you care to join us?" Claire invited, with a side smirk at Andrew. William agreed, and they did another turn around the circuit of the promenade deck. Andrew led them purposely to the end of the deck overlooking the stern. There were some sailors at work coiling ropes, and a couple of passengers sitting on a bench. He was disappointed not to see Matthew. He turned away so Claire or William wouldn't see any emotion on his face.

Nearby, the bugler sounded the call for dinner, and the trio broke up with a promise to meet in the reception room for a drink before dinner. Andrew remained behind at the rail, watching them walk away. He meant what he had said to Claire, that he wasn't frightened by her threats.

I'll figure a way out of this mess, Andrew thought as he walked back to his cabin.

Andrew was sitting in a corner of the reception room with a glass of whisky in his hand, listening to the orchestra play, when he saw Claire and William coming down the stairs. They paused, as if surveying the assembled ladies and gentlemen, and then they saw Andrew and walked toward him to sit down. Claire halted halfway and engaged in conversation with Lucile Duff Gordon, who was standing with her husband, and William pulled up a chair next to Andrew.

"I hear you two had a lovers' spat this afternoon. Please tell me everything's all right, old chap."

"Everything's all right, William," Andrew said the words without enthusiasm, but William pretended not to notice. He leaned in closer to Andrew.

"I certainly hope so. I know the quarrels between lovers don't last long. You'll be old friends by the end of dinner." William smiled.

Andrew shook his head and turned away. He listened to a conversation behind him between two couples.

"We'll be motoring down to Philadelphia to visit my sister and back to New York in time for the reception…"

"Old man, are you even listening to me?" William asked.

Andrew turned back to William. "I'm sorry, I was distracted for a second. What were you saying?"

William frowned. "I was saying that I hope you and I would have some time to ourselves before you slip on the old ball and chain." William laughed, but Andrew didn't find it the least bit funny. He wondered how much of his conversation with Claire had made it back to her brother.

"I think Claire's coming over. Shall we all go to dinner?" Andrew got up, happy to have a distraction.

William remained seated, frowning up at him.

Dinner was a very subdued affair between Andrew, William, and Claire. Claire and her brother chattered amiably among themselves and ignored Andrew altogether. Andrew finally gave up thinking about them and focused his attention on Matthew.

If they had been back in Edinburgh or London, Andrew could have telephoned the Elliot family solicitor and asked him to help Matthew, even if he had to face his father's wrath, or he could have taken the train down to London and tracked down Lord Carson to sort out the whole thing. He suddenly felt a light touch on his shoulder.

"Hello, Andrew. I was just asking if you would like to play some chess later this evening," Mr. Millet said to him.

Andrew smiled. "Sure, I'll join you in a while." He felt the table under his elbow shake, and he looked across to Claire and William, who both sat staring at him, faces like stone.

Chapter Twelve

Matthew was standing on his toes, straining to look out the porthole, when he heard the doorknob turn. He looked around and saw a steward letting Andrew into the room.

"Come on. I persuaded them to let you go outside." Andrew smiled and motioned for Matthew to follow him. When they reached the well deck leading to the stern, Andrew turned to the steward who had accompanied them.

"Will you leave us alone, please?"

"It's against orders, sir."

"I'm sure it is, but we can't exactly run away, can we? I promise faithfully to return Cinderella home by midnight," Andrew said, reaching out to place something in the steward's hand. The steward looked at it, smiled, and walked away, leaving them alone.

Andrew led Matthew to a bench overlooking the ocean, and for a while they sat watching the foaming trail made by the propellers stretch into the night and fade away. Andrew reached into his pocket and offered Matthew a cigarette from a silver case.

"Thanks," Matthew said, taking one and lighting it. He blew the smoke over their heads. There was another silence, and then Matthew spoke, "I don't want to get you in trouble coming down here like this."

"It doesn't matter. All that matters is that I wanted to see you, and nothing can keep me away," Andrew said, thinking briefly about Claire's threat.

"I'm happy you did. I was thinking about you all day."

"Me too, Matthew," Andrew said. He leaned back on the bench and looked up at the starlit sky above his head. Matthew followed his gaze upward.

"You know, Matthew, I wish this voyage would last forever. I wish I could turn the ship around and go back to England," Andrew said.

"Are you sure you know the way?" Matthew turned his head toward Andrew and smiled.

"I could guess the direction, but I think it's better to go forward rather than backward," Andrew said with a grin. He leaned his head back and sighed.

"What's on your mind, Andrew? I can tell there is something. Tell me," Matthew said softly. He leaned on Andrew, one hand resting gently on Andrew's.

Andrew lit a cigarette and blew the smoke over the rail. He pointed over toward the lighted windows of the first-class decks. "My fiancée and her brother are playing cards in the lounge at this moment, if you want to know."

"Your fiancée. I had no idea."

"It wasn't my idea either. It was my father's, and he believes it'll be the cure for what ails me."

"Do you love her?" Matthew asked.

Andrew looked straight ahead of him over the rail, not answering the question. Instead, he said, "If I don't marry her, then I lose my inheritance, and if I do, then I'll be tied down to a woman I don't trust and don't care for, and I'll have to provide for her shiftless brother as well. No amount of money is worth that. There are so many options in life, Matthew."

"I'm sorry, Andrew, truly." Matthew pulled himself even closer to Andrew.

Andrew looked ahead into the dark.

"Why can't I be like you, Matthew, go to America, or join the Army like my older brother, pursue my dreams just like you are? I studied at Oxford, and for a man supposedly so smart I don't feel that clever. If I was, then I wouldn't be in this situation right now."

"All those things are possible. I know it all sounds philosophical from a man being sent back to England for a crime he didn't commit, but why don't you do all those things? I think you have more courage than you realize. It took a lot of courage to come down here and spend time with me. You can do anything you want, Andrew, believe me."

Andrew looked at him sideways, amazed at his words.

"In a few months I'll be tied down, Matthew, and then I go to work or something, and then come the children, and any hopes or dreams I have will be nothing more than a puff of smoke," Andrew noted sadly, but then he straightened. "I came down here to cheer you up, not to bore you with my tale of woe. Do you play chess? Checkers?" Andrew asked.

"I'm glad you talked to me, and yes, I play a good game of checkers.

"Tell me something, Andrew, and be honest. Are you happy?"

"I can never be happier than I am right now with you, in the middle of the North Atlantic Ocean on the grandest ship in the world. You know it's possible that one day airplanes will fly across from Europe to America, but nothing will ever be like this, like being on the *Titanic*." Andrew sighed.

"I'm sorry I spoiled it by asking about your emotions. I would like this to last forever, Andrew," Matthew said, looking from Andrew down to his hands.

"No, you didn't spoil anything. I did, by bringing up my fiancée,"

Andrew said apologetically.

Matthew smiled. "Then let's forget her right now, shall we? We have these few days at sea. Let's not allow your fiancée or her brother or Lord Carson to ruin our time together." Matthew leaned forward and looked down at the ocean churned up by the propellers. Andrew followed his gaze, and together they *stared at the endless expanse of stars and ocean moving past them.*

Finally, Andrew sat back. "Then come on down to the smoking room. We'll have some ale and play a couple of games," he said, standing and pulling Matthew up with him.

"I don't think I'm allowed…"

"I'm allowing it, and if your friend Tom is working, he'll be glad to see you. Now come on," Andrew said, walking toward the stairs to the well deck. Matthew followed him.

Andrew looked briefly upward to the first-class deck. He saw people strolling past and looking down on third-class, but he couldn't see their faces, only outlines. He and Matthew walked past them and into the smoking room.

They found an empty table next to a group of boisterous men playing a game of cards, and sat down. Tom saw them and came over, smiling, happy to see them together.

"I'm glad they let you out, mate. What can I bring you two?" Tom asked.

"A couple of glasses of ale," Andrew said. While Tom went to get the drinks, Andrew found a checkerboard and set it up. Tom returned with the drinks and excused himself to help a group seated nearby. Andrew watched across the table as Matthew picked up his glass and took a swig.

"Andrew, I want to thank you for this. I hope you don't get into trouble for me."

"You let me worry about that. Just enjoy the ale. Now come on, you make the first move," Andrew said, pointing down at the board.

Matthew slid one of his pieces across, and Andrew countered with his own move, then waited, staring silently across the table into Matthew's eyes.

"What are you thinking about over there?"

"I know you're from Ireland, but aside from that, I know little else about you."

"Ha, there isn't much to tell." Matthew suddenly seemed shy.

Andrew grinned at him across the table. "Were you a wild little boy who always got into trouble?"

"Well, now, you'll have to be asking others about that. I think I was a good lad, aside from sneaking into the loft of my parents' barn with my chums to look at bawdy pictures," Matthew said with a sly grin and chuckled. Andrew laughed along with him.

"Any brothers and sisters? What about your parents?"

"I have a brother in Belfast. My parents passed away a few months ago…" Matthew said quietly.

"I'm sorry, Matthew." Andrew wanted to reach out and touch his friend, but the room was fairly crowded, so he smiled instead, looking down at the table. Matthew nodded.

"It's all right. I'm getting used to it now, but I still miss them," Matthew said.

To change the suddenly somber mood, Andrew asked, "What are your plans when we reach America?" He watched Matthew move a piece on the board.

"I'll get on a train to Texas and get a job on a ranch. I worked on my parents' small farm. That will help me," Matthew said confidently, looking into Andrew's face with a faint smile.

Matthew moved his checker one space and captured Andrew's.

"I may win this game if you're not careful, Andrew. I should tell you again that I'm quite good at checkers."

"Is that so? Prove it." Andrew smiled. Matthew laughed and proceeded to take more of Andrew's checker pieces from the board.

"Ha, I told you. You'll have to request a rematch."

"I intend to beat you next game," Andrew said. It felt good to sit across from Matthew and see him smile and look at the way he tilted his head to one side while he pondered a move. Matthew reached for his glass of ale and took another drink. "What are you thinking about, Matthew? You look as if you're trying to figure me out or something."

"Maybe I am, mate. I know so little about you, and I opened myself up to you about Lord Carson and everything…"

"What do you want to know that I might not have shared?"

"Anything…" Matthew shrugged.

Andrew drank from his glass and then set it down. "Well, I studied history at Oxford, and I hope one day to write a study of ancient Sumer, one of the earliest known civilizations. Boring stuff to everyone else, I'm afraid."

"I would like to hear about it sometime. What about when you were a little boy?" Matthew asked.

Andrew laughed. "I played tricks on my governess and blamed it on the ghosts."

"Ghosts?"

"My family house in Edinburgh is haunted, but those are stories for later. What else can I tell you? I read a lot of books, play cricket quite well, I can drive an automobile, and at my family's estate in the north of Scotland, I have a couple of horses that I like to ride when we stay there in the fall for the shooting. One day I'll show you the place," Andrew said.

Matthew was clearly impressed, and he said, "Is there a castle, like the kind I used to see in the Irish countryside with turrets and a moat and all that?"

"It's more of a manor house, and has turrets but no moat. It was built in the early eighteenth century to replace another dwelling that burned down; I don't think it ever saw a battle. There is an actual castle nearby," Andrew said. "What about you, Matthew? I know you want to become a cowboy out in Texas, but there must be other things that interest you…" Andrew spoke over the rim of his glass.

Matthew slid another checker into a space. He looked around the crowded room. "I wish I was still a steward. It looks like *they* could use some help. I'll wager you never thought about doing anything like that?"

Andrew smiled, got up off the bench, and removed his jacket. "Oh yeah, I might surprise you." He laughed. Andrew walked over to Tom and said something in his ear. Matthew saw a look of disbelief on Tom's face, and then he motioned for Andrew to follow him.

A few minutes later the door to the pantry swung open. Tom came out first, followed by Andrew, wearing a white mess jacket and carrying a cloth over his right arm.

He smiled in Matthew's direction, and then he stopped to lean over a table of men wearing workers' caps and smoking. The men looked at Andrew with the same shocked expression Tom had, seeing a well-dressed man standing over them and asking if they wanted a round of drinks. Matthew could hear their voices over the noise.

"A couple of pints and a whisky… off with you and be lively," one man said, slapping his palm on the table.

"Yes, sir, right away." Andrew grinned and bowed from the waist, then walked back to the pantry. He returned a few minutes later with a tray laden with drinks balanced on his hand. He walked over to the table and set them down. Tom was right behind him.

"Sit down, sir, you ought not to be doing this. If one of the officers or the chief steward comes in…" Tom cautioned.

Andrew returned to the table and sat back down with Matthew. "How did I do?"

"Not too bad."

"Not too bad? I think I did quite well for my first experience being a steward. If my father cuts me out of his will, I can get work as a steward."

"All right, Andrew, you were better at it the first time than I was." Matthew laughed over the checkerboard as he jumped three more pieces, removing them from the board. "You're a rotten checker player, mate, because I win," Matthew said proudly as he took the last of Andrew's checkers and put them off to the side.

"I demand a rematch." Andrew grabbed his checkers and placed them back on their squares. Andrew and Matthew stared at each other over the rims of their glasses of ale. Andrew set his down. "Since you won the first game, make the first move," Andrew said.

Matthew smiled and moved across the board. While Andrew took the next turn, Matthew glanced over and saw Tom on the side of the room; he nodded in his friend's direction.

It was eleven-thirty when they went outside. They leaned on the rail of the well deck, looking at the stars. Andrew stood close to Matthew, feeling the warmth of Matthew's body next to his.

"Thank you, Andrew, for tonight."

"It won't be much to look back on when the voyage is over, will it? Not very memorable."

"You're wrong, Andrew. We'll remember this night, *this voyage* for a very long time."

"Will we? I know a game of checkers and a pint of ale isn't much. If we were in first class, we might have gone to the after dinner concert and a stroll on the promenade."

"That sounds nice, but I enjoyed this more than a concert or a walk."

"So did I," Andrew said quietly, rubbing his hands on the leg of his pants.

Matthew watched him for a second, and then asked, "What's on your mind? You look like you want to say something."

"I want to say—" At that moment footsteps sounded close, and the steward stopped in front of them. Andrew swore under his breath. "I guess it's time for your coach to become a pumpkin," he said, disappointed.

Matthew kicked the tip of his shoe on the deck. "I wish we could have had longer. There is so much to say. I…" Matthew reached out, and they shook hands.

Though Andrew would have loved to kiss him, it wasn't possible. They stared into each other's eyes, not saying a word until the steward cleared his throat, reminding them of his presence.

"I'll see you tomorrow after church services. Maybe they'll let me bring you up here again." Andrew looked to the steward hopefully, and the man's response was a shrug.

"Good night," they said in unison.

Andrew remained standing where he was while Matthew and the steward walked away.

Andrew's steps were slow as he made his way back up to first class and then into the smoking room. He found Frank Millet, John Jacob Astor, and Archie Butt seated at a table where the chess pieces had already been set up. The gentlemen greeted Andrew cordially, and two of them shifted their chairs to make room for Andrew across from Mr. Millet.

While Andrew waited for Mr. Millet to make the opening move, he felt eyes on him, so he looked up. Through the cigar smoke, William was staring at him from a chair in the corner. Andrew tried not to focus on him or what could possibly be on his mind.

"It's your move," Mr. Millet said.

Andrew made his opening move and tried to ignore William, who remained sitting in the same place until finally he got up and walked out through the revolving door.

Andrew attempted to remain focused on the game, but between moves he thought, Claire must have told him about our conversation this afternoon, and he was here waiting to fight me for his sister's honor. Well, if that's what he wants—

"Wake up, Andrew. It's your move."

"I'm sorry, sir." Andrew smiled, and then after pondering for a moment, moved one of his chess pieces on the board.

Matthew lay on his bunk, with the wool blanket pulled up to his chin, staring above him and savoring the time he had spent with Andrew that night, even though he wished it had been longer. He turned his head, and in the dark saw the faint crack of light from under the cabin door. If it hadn't been locked, he would have sneaked up to Andrew's cabin in first class and spent the night, but as soon as the steward had brought him back, the key had turned in the lock.

He closed his eyes and tried to imagine Andrew next to him, feeling his hands wrapped around him and warming him in the chilly room. He fell asleep dreaming about him and Andrew, riding horses together across the wide-open plains of Texas.

Andrew was alone on the first-class deck overlooking the bow and feeling the spray on his face as the *Titanic* raced ahead. There was only the sound of the ocean, the faint throb of the engines, and the creaking of gears. He looked at his pocket watch. It was officially Sunday, the fourteenth. He remained on deck for a few minutes longer before he stifled a yawn and decided it was time to go to bed.

Andrew returned to his cabin, got undressed and into bed, and pulled the soft comforter over himself. He lay in the dark thinking about Matthew before sleep claimed him.

Chapter Thirteen

Sunday, April fourteen, 1912

Andrew woke up, squinting at the stream of light coming through a part in the curtains. He stretched and then sat up. After a few minutes, he finally threw the covers aside and got out of bed.

Bathed and dressed, he picked up his book and went into the reading room until it was time for breakfast and then church services in the dining saloon.

Andrew was sitting in his usual chair in front of the large window, absorbed in the adventures of Sir Walter Scott's characters in old England, when he heard someone come in, walk across the room, and sit down next to him.

"Good morning, William."

"Andrew," came the curt response.

Andrew closed his book and got up. He took a couple of steps forward before he turned around and said, "Let's go for a walk on deck." He led the way out of the reading room, up the grand staircase, and out onto the boat deck. They walked, then came to a stop along the rail looking out over the ocean. Andrew lit a cigarette and offered one to William, who refused.

"Whom have you been meeting down in steerage? I know there's someone, and so does my sister. We saw you last night."

"I don't owe you any explanations."

"You owe something to my sister. She's your fiancée."

"I don't owe anything. I've been doing some thinking, and I've decided to remain in America, maybe settle in Texas or somewhere farther west, and write, or maybe get a job." Andrew said.

"We'll see about that," William said, rubbing his hands together.

Andrew smiled, because the gesture reminded him of the scoundrels in moving pictures.

"I wouldn't laugh if I were you. Do you want your father to find out what you're up to, consorting with a steward, of all people? *A steward.*" William spat out the two words like a curse.

"Claire showed me the wire yesterday, so go ahead and send it," Andrew said.

William leaned over the rail and stared down into the waves curling from the *Titanic*'s side. "I don't think you realize what kind of situation you're in, that *we're* in, old chap."

Here it comes. "What are you talking about, William?"

"There are a lot of people depending on this marriage. You keep your shameful secret undercover from the world, thus keeping your inheritance secure—"

"And you keep hidden the fact that there is no Sir Cliverford, no island estate, and no money. Should I go on, William?" Andrew said, noticing that William was looking uncomfortable, but William recovered himself quickly.

"Do you want to see my sister and me cast out on the street or in prison? Is that what you want?"

"No. What I want is…" Andrew sighed out over the water, suddenly shivering as a bitterly cold wind hit them both. "It's getting colder. Perhaps, we should continue this discussion at another time when we're calmer and we can come to a mutual agreement," Andrew said.

"Claire should be present also," William said.

"That's only fair, but let's do this before we reach New York," Andrew said, pulling his overcoat tighter around his body.

William nodded. They were walking back toward the entrance to the grand staircase when William stopped Andrew and pulled him aside.

"I suppose you know that I have feelings for you, old man?"

"Well, you weren't very subtle that night at my father's home, but I'm your sister's fiancée, as you and everyone else keep reminding me, so if you think that entitles you to sneak into my rooms in the night, then you're much mistaken. I have no interest in you. Thank you, anyway," Andrew replied curtly.

"That's all you have to say to me? Well, we shall see who has the last word." William laughed.

Andrew tried to push past him, but William blocked his way inside. Andrew caught him by the arm. "Your sister and my parents would love to know about your secret, William Bennett." Andrew tried to remain calm, but even in the icy air, he could feel heat rising to his face.

"They would never believe you, a known poof."

"We'll see about that, William. Now move aside," Andrew said, releasing William.

They stared into each other's eyes, and William was the first to relent. He stepped out of Andrew's way.

"Come down to join your sister and me for breakfast and church services, and we'll say nothing more about any of this until later," Andrew said.

"Thank you, but I would rather stay out here and walk for a while," William said, drawing the collar of his coat tighter.

Matthew watched from the edge of the bunk as a steward removed the breakfast tray, exited the room, and shut the door. A cold breeze whipped through the porthole, and he got off the bunk to shut it. Instead of sitting back down, he paced back and forth in front of the door. Suddenly he heard the click of a key in the lock.

"Andrew?" he said happily, but his hope was dashed when a tall man with dark, thinning hair and a moustache entered the room. The door closed again, and they were alone. They stood eyeing each other, and Matthew asked, "Who are you?"

"That's exactly what I was going to say to you. Sit down." The man motioned for Matthew to sit on the edge of the bunk.

Matthew was unsure, but he complied. He looked up at the man, who began to pace in front of him.

"I'm William Bennett, by the way, and you're Matthew?"

"Aye, but how did you know that?"

"I asked a crewman. They know everyone's business, and for a couple of pounds, they'll tell you all you want to hear."

"All right, you know who I am, but what do you want?"

"I'm here to tell you to leave Andrew Elliot alone. Is that clear?"

"Who are you to tell me what to do, mate?" Matthew asked, and William stopped moving as he bent close to Matthew's face.

"I'll tell you who I am—a damned bit more important to Andrew than you are. You see, we have a special relationship. Yes, Andrew and I are quite close, and I won't have some working-class boy come between us," William said.

"There's nothing between you. Andrew told me so," Matthew stammered.

William laughed. "He told you that? That's just like him. Well, I'm afraid you've been played for a fool, boy." William smoothed a crease in his pants and began to pace again.

Matthew remained seated on the bunk, stunned by William's words.

Andrew is making a fool of me? It can't be possible.

"Why did you come down here to tell me that?"

"I thought it was my duty as a gentleman to see you and tell you to keep away from him. Though I guess while you're cooped up in here, you can't exactly go running to Andrew, now can you?" William said.

Matthew knew that perhaps Andrew or a steward had provided this man with information. He felt the cabin suddenly become very small and much colder.

"He could return at any time," Matthew informed him.

"I wouldn't put any confidence in that, my boy."

"I'm not your 'boy',' so stop calling me that," Matthew snapped. "Whatever you want. You're going to send him a message telling him you don't want to see him ever again."

"If I don't?" Matthew managed to say.

William looked at the signet ring on his finger, concentrating hard, and then lifted his head. "Then I'll see some disagreeable accident befalls you before we reach New York. Also, I can pay someone to prevent Andrew from coming down here. He needs to remember his place," William spat.

"Your threats don't frighten me," Matthew said.

William laughed again, and he opened the flap of his coat, revealing the shining butt of a revolver.

Matthew stared at it, pretending not to be disturbed by the sight.

William covered it up again. He strode across the room to the door, ready to knock. He turned around to look at Matthew. "Remember to keep in mind what I said." William knocked on the door, and the crewman waiting in the hall opened the door to let him out.

Matthew sat motionless after he was gone. He stared at the floor until the pattern in the tile was embedded in his brain.

Not see Andrew? How can I do that? How did this man find out about us, and what is this special relationship they supposedly share?

He replayed in his mind all the time he'd spent with Andrew and recalled all their conversations. Andrew had mentioned a fiancée. *Could this be the brother he once spoke about?*

Matthew lay on his back, pounding the mattress with his fist.

Andrew and Claire were sitting with Frank Millet and a couple from Michigan when William came to the table.

"I'm sorry to keep you waiting. I had business to take care of." William smiled in Claire's direction.

Andrew saw the looks they exchanged. He glanced away from them when he heard someone mention that they would probably see some icebergs later that night or Monday morning.

"I heard it from the chairman of the White Star Line. He's sitting over there. He told me that they received some reports from other ships ahead of *Titanic* passing icebergs, one yesterday and a couple of them this morning," the man from Michigan said, and his wife corroborated his story.

"That would explain the colder temperatures on deck," Andrew said.

"The thought of being among bergs makes me nervous…" Claire said over the rim of her coffee cup. She was about to continue her sentence when Captain Smith, who had overheard her, stopped at the table, all smiles.

"There's no need to worry, Miss. We're speeding up to get as far ahead of the danger as possible. If you'll all excuse me." He bowed to everyone at the table and walked toward the entrance to the dining room.

"See, there's nothing to worry about. The *Titanic* is unsinkable, anyway," William said.

Andrew sat over his eggs and bacon, listening, and he was relieved when the last plates were cleared away and he could pass the time until Sunday services sitting in the lounge with his book.

Going up the grand staircase, he saw Thomas Andrews standing on the landing making notes in a book. He smiled and nodded when Andrew approached him. Andrew wanted to stop and talk to him, but Mr. Andrews looked preoccupied with finding things to perfect.

"Hello, Mr. Elliot."

"Good morning, Mr. Andrews," Andrew said as he passed up the stairs to his cabin. He picked up his book, and then, after closing his door behind him, Andrew went to sit in the Louis XVI lounge by the fireplace until it was time to go down for church services.

Andrew sat in the front row of chairs arranged for the Sunday service, and next to him sat Claire and William. In front of them stood Captain Smith, flanked by four of his senior officers. He closed the *Book of Common Prayer*, which he held in his hand, and addressed the assembly.

"May the Lord bless and keep us. The Lord make his face shine upon us and be gracious to us. Amen."

Andrew and the others assembled for the service responded softly, "Amen."

"Now, let us close with 'Eternal Father Strong to Save'," Captain Smith said. There was the sound of pages being turned in books. The pianist began to play, and the assembly sang...

"*O hear us when we cry to Thee for those in peril on the sea...*" the song concluded. There was the usual rustle of people moving about and stopping to chat as they drifted toward the reception room. Andrew was almost out of the room when Claire and William blocked his path.

"Where are you going in such a rush?" Claire asked.

"I have some business to take care of, Claire."

"Is it that important? We were hoping you would be up for another game of cards or joining me down at the swimming bath again," William spoke with a slight smile.

"Maybe I'll join you later. I have to be going," Andrew said, taking a few more steps toward the door.

William caught up with him and whispered tersely in his ear, "I hope you're not going to *him*."

"If I am, what's that to you or Claire?" Andrew said. Not waiting for an answer, he left the room before either could say anything more.

Andrew stepped out on deck and discovered it was even colder than it had been earlier, and there were even fewer people out walking. He went quickly inside, where it was warmer, and made his way down to the third-class cabins. He found a steward, who led him to where Matthew was held and unlocked the door to let Andrew in.

Matthew was sitting on the edge of the bunk. When Andrew came in, Matthew looked away from him and didn't return Andrew's greeting or his warm smile.

"What's wrong, Matthew?"

"Nothing's wrong. Why are you here, anyway?" Matthew sounded slightly tense.

"I promised I would come to see you this morning," Andrew said, sitting next to Matthew on the bunk.

"I had another visitor this morning. Who's William?"

"William was here? What did he want to see you about?" Andrew said, his voice anxious.

"He said that I was not to see you again…" Matthew stopped. He reached out to Andrew, and they held each other for a minute or two.

"Listen to me, Matthew, whatever he said to you, I wouldn't believe a word of it. He's just as bad as his sister," Andrew said.

"That's the brother you mentioned?" Matthew said, to which Andrew nodded without saying a word.

Andrew felt himself shaking with anger at someone like William invading his private world.

Matthew hugged him closer. "What if he hurts you, Andrew? He seems capable of it."

"I can take care of myself, but I won't let him hurt you," Andrew said.

Matthew got up from the bunk and lifted his head to look out the porthole at the brilliant blue sky. Andrew watched him, and then got up to join him.

"It looks like a grand day, doesn't it?" Matthew said, silently longing to be outside on deck to enjoy it.

"It is, but it's getting colder," Andrew observed.

Matthew sighed. They both turned away from the porthole and faced each other. Andrew took Matthew's face in his hands for a kiss; they barely heard the knock on the door in time to quickly step away from each other.

When the steward entered to let Andrew out, Matthew was sitting in the bunk and Andrew was near the door. In the hallway, Andrew looked back over his shoulder.

"I'll be back later on." Then the door closed.

Chapter Fourteen

Despite the bitter cold afternoon, Andrew found a deck chair on the boat deck and sat, pulling his coat tighter around his body.

I can't go through with this marriage now. I couldn't live with her or that parasite of a brother that I don't trust. I'll have to tell them before we dock that the wedding is off. And though I respect my father, he will have to know and understand that I'm staying in America with or without his blessing.

After a few more minutes in the cold, Andrew stood up and headed back inside. He stepped through the door leading to the grand staircase and was crossing the landing to the stairs when he met Margaret Brown, wrapped in a sable coat and matching hat, coming up the stairs. She smiled up at Andrew as he was about to step down, and he paused and waited for her.

"Good day, young man. It must be cold out there. Your face and ears are glowing," she said loudly.

"I was thinking about something, and I just sat down out there and lost track of the time."

"I would get some hot tea and buttered toast in you right away. We'll chat more later, dear," Mrs. Brown called over her shoulder, and went through the door leading outside.

Andrew remained where he was until the door closed; something told him that maybe she wouldn't mind the temperature out on deck. He chuckled and walked down the stairs.

Andrew returned to his cabin to change clothes and grab his book, and then he went to the reading room. He found his usual chair by the window unoccupied and sat down. A steward brought him tea, buttered toast and marmalade. It helped warm his body.

In between paragraphs of his book and the notes he was making, he would lift his eyes from the page and look out the window. He saw Bruce Ismay, whom someone had pointed out to him earlier as chairman of the shipping line, talking to two women and showing them a piece of paper he had removed from his pocket. He saw William and Claire strolling past the window, and they paused to nod at him before they walked on, engaged in some sort of deep conversation. Nearby, he could hear the string orchestra softly playing a Strauss waltz.

Andrew focused on his book once again, but he found his mind wandering as he thought about Matthew. He had never felt like this about anyone; not even Robert had occupied his thoughts so much, or touched him or shared things with him, as Matthew had in just a few short days.

Even though there had been no confrontations or bitter tears between himself, Claire, her brother, or his family, Andrew wanted Matthew to know he was willing to fight to stay with him, even if it meant prison and scandal.

Matthew nervously paced the small cabin. He hadn't thought about Lord Carson or Daniel but twice since he met Andrew, but now he had time to dwell on them. He had hoped not to see either one again. He sat back down on the edge of the bunk, gazing at the tiled floor.

No doubt there'll be some kind of trial, and Lord Carson will be in the box accusing me of being a typical Irishman out to bring down the British Empire, but it's not true… I wish I'd never met him. Andrew is the only good thing that's happened during this whole ordeal, and for him I'm thankful.

Matthew got off the bed and went over to the porthole. He stretched to look out at the ocean passing by a few feet below and the blue and gold sky. Someone would come soon and bring his tea, and if he could persuade them, maybe they would let him up on deck to watch the sunset, and maybe he would catch a glimpse of Andrew as he passed by.

"I can only hope…"

The bugler sounded dinner just as Andrew finished another chapter in his book. He would have to go down and dine with Claire and William, laugh and smile, and make plans for New York.

Andrew was looking in the mirror and fixing his tie when a knock sounded on his door.

"I've come to walk down with you," William called out to him from the hallway.

"I'll be out in a minute," Andrew tried not to sound disappointed. He paused before he opened the door, taking a final look in the mirror to make sure he was smiling, and then he went out.

William clutched Andrew tightly around the bicep, so there was no escape. Andrew winced and pulled himself free.

"Come on, old chap. Claire's waiting for us in the reception room." William grinned. Andrew frowned and didn't say anything. "Relax and play the game. It'll only be easier if you do."

"If it's a game, then I'm not enjoying it," Andrew said bitterly. He walked away ahead of William.

The reception room was crowded with the latest fashions from Paris and handsome men in white tie and tails, but Andrew couldn't concentrate on them. He felt like he was moving slowly down the stairs and through the crowd to where Claire sat sipping a glass of wine on a sofa beneath a tapestry. In the corner, the orchestra was playing a Victor Herbert melody *I'm Falling in Love with Someone*.

"Andrew, you look handsome tonight," Claire gushed.

Andrew could only give her a half smile and a nod. William stood behind, boxing him in. Just then, a man and two women walking toward the dining saloon stepped between Andrew and Claire. The distraction was enough for Andrew to move away from the pair. He went into the dining room, and seeing a steward, he stopped the man and took him aside to present an idea that had suddenly come to him.

"That's very irregular, sir, and I don't think it can be done," the steward informed him.

Andrew reached into his pocket and pulled out a piece of paper, which he pressed into the man's hand. "This says it's possible." Andrew gave the man a slight smile, and the steward's eyes lit up when he saw the ten-pound note.

Matthew was sitting on the bunk, and he was startled to hear the key turning in the lock.

Is it time for someone to bring tea already? An hour and a half earlier, a steward had come to allow Matthew to bathe and shave, and it felt better not to be so grubby.

The door opened, and he was surprised to see Andrew dressed in a black bow tie and jacket. Behind him, a steward pushed a cart with covered dishes, napkins, silverware, and crystal—a sight never before seen in third-class on any ship.

"Dinner is served, m'lord," Andrew said with the same drawn-out words of a butler. He lifted the cover off one of the dishes to reveal sirloin of beef with roasted potatoes and green beans, and not on the plain third-class plates, but on first-class china. The steward wheeled the cart into the space between the bunks. Andrew sat on one and Matthew sat facing him.

"I... I can't believe you're doing this, Andrew. Will you get in trouble?" Matthew asked, eyeing the array of food Andrew had brought in.

Andrew waited until the steward left before he answered Matthew's question. "I might get in trouble, but I couldn't let you dine alone in this tiny room. All that's missing is music, but I didn't bring my gramophone on this trip, and the orchestra is occupied elsewhere." Andrew lifted the cover off the other dish.

"Thank you..." Matthew stopped before he said *I love you.* Maybe it was too soon to tell Andrew how he felt.

Andrew lifted a hand. "No talking right now. Eat first and we'll talk over coffee." He pointed to the coffee pot and cups on the second shelf of the cart.

They ate their dinner and then relaxed over the coffee.

"If we were in other circumstances, we might go for a walk after this meal, even if it is a lot colder on deck than it was," Andrew said.

"I'm still wondering how you pulled this off," Matthew said.

"Don't worry about that. Just enjoy it," Andrew said with a smile. Matthew looked up from the coffee cups and into Andrew's face.

"I thought I would never see you again," Matthew said quietly. Andrew moved the serving cart aside and sat on the bunk next to

Matthew. Their hands, close to touching, felt warm. "I couldn't stay away from you, Matthew, not even if I wanted to." Matthew moved closer to him and reached out his hand to take Andrew's. "What are we going to do? He looked like the kind of man who won't stop until I'm out of the way and you're married to his sister." Matthew was anxious.

"Don't be afraid of William. He can't harm you, and if he does..." Andrew slammed a fist on the table.

"He could hurt, maybe even kill you, Andrew. I only met him the once, and he looked like the type." Matthew was genuinely worried.

Andrew looked thoughtful. "Now, it's my turn to give you some confidence, Matthew. Don't fret about William. We're alone here together, aren't we?" Andrew leaned in closer to him. "Now, I'll tell you what we're going to do. First thing tomorrow morning, I'm going to send a wire to my family solicitor and see if he can persuade Lord Carson to change his attitude, and then when the *Titanic* reaches New York, I'm going with you to Texas. As for William and Claire, well, leave them to me."

"I can't believe what I'm hearing. You want to go with me to Texas? But what about your ambitions? I can't be selfish..."

"What about them? I can write my book in Texas. Bloody hell, it may even enhance my writing. This is the second decade of the twentieth century—anything is possible. You told me that. It's given us this grand ship we're sailing on, hasn't it? Then don't worry about what I'm going to do," Andrew said.

He leaned over and gave Matthew a kiss, softly at first. Gradually it became more passionate, until Matthew began to respond with a fiery kiss of his own. Andrew pulled him closer, and Matthew reached up, undid Andrew's tie, and tossed it on the floor.

Sunday, April fourteen, 1912, ten p.m.

They lay holding each other on the bed, reluctant to let go. Andrew kissed Matthew on the back of the neck and whispered into his ear, "I love you."

"Me too," Matthew whispered back, his voice husky. He shifted on the bed and swung his legs over the edge.

Andrew reached out to him. "Where are you going?"

"I'm getting some water. Want some?" He leaned over and kissed Andrew again before he stood up.

Andrew sat up with the blanket around his waist and watched Matthew standing at the washbasin filling a glass with water.

After a moment, Andrew reached for his jacket hanging from a peg. He pulled out his pocket watch and looked at it. Andrew got out of bed, then came over to put his arms around Matthew's waist and hold him close.

Matthew was reluctant to ask, but he said, "Do you have to go?"

"I'm afraid so. The steward is coming back in fifteen minutes. I wish I didn't have to go," Andrew said, slowly getting dressed.

"Then stay with me. Don't break the magic spell we feel right now."

"I'll be back for breakfast, and then we're going to see the captain," Andrew said.

Matthew still couldn't bear to have him leave, but he got dressed and was fastening the last button when there was a knock on the door.

The steward came in and found them standing on opposite sides of the room. He addressed Andrew. "I'm afraid time's up, sir." The steward moved the serving cart with the used dishes into the hall.

"I understand." Andrew followed the crewman to the door, but he paused to turn and smile at Matthew.

"Tomorrow, we'll go outside for a walk on deck."

"Until tomorrow, then," Matthew said before the door closed and separated them.

The harsh cold kept everyone else indoors, but it didn't bother Andrew. He still felt the warmth of Matthew's touch as he leaned on the rail. Looking down, he noticed the ocean was unusually flat and calm, and the waves tossing from the side of *Titanic* as it plowed on through the night created the only disturbance. It was almost hypnotic, and in the foam, he caught glimpses of himself and Matthew wrapped around each other, loving each other. He had shared love with Robert, but this was different; there was more tenderness, more passion, more spark than he'd ever felt before.

Andrew prayed that Matthew would always feel the same for him, that in time he would forget Lord Carson and would see that not every man was out to use him and either cast him off or cause problems for him.

Andrew's love was not the syrupy sentiment of popular songs, but he felt it was true and more honest. Even if his father had him thrown in jail or cut off his money, he could face anything. He would have to use that courage to face William and Claire in the morning. Andrew checked his pocket watch, and it was just before eleven o'clock.

He went inside to the smoking room and found Frank Millet, Archie Butt, and two other gentlemen deep in conversation. They didn't seem to notice his presence, so he wandered toward the lounge and looked inside through the oak doors. William and Claire were playing cards together and talking animatedly about something in hushed voices. They didn't notice him, so he went to his cabin to read and write letters.

He started a letter, but in ten minutes, he wasn't able to get past the words: *fourteen April 1912. Dearest Aunt Olivia.* He set the paper, pen, and inkwell aside and decided that reading would be better.

Andrew turned on the space heater, picked up his book, and settled back on the sofa.

Matthew wished Andrew could have stayed with him. They had so much to talk about. True, they'd talked in bed after their lovemaking, but they were both aware the spell would be broken by the arrival of the steward to let Andrew out.

Then the steward came. Now Matthew lay on his back on the bed, his hands behind his head, staring at the ceiling.

He had shared with Andrew before he left, the persistent feeling that William would come back, and this time his threats might become real, or that Lord Carson, being a noble, might try to make him sound like a common thief. Andrew had laughed and tried to calm his fears by telling him that Lord Carson was in Europe, and William was up above in first class. He might have come down to threaten, but that would be the extent of it.

"I wish I shared your confidence," Matthew had said to him.

Andrew turned, raised himself up on an elbow, and gently touched his face. "You worry too much, Matthew."

"It's probably my biggest weakness, but then you're not being sent back to England to face…"

"Don't think about that," Andrew had said, pressing his finger to Matthew's lips before stealing a quick kiss.

Matthew pulled himself up in bed and put his feet on the floor. The cabin was uncomfortably warm, so he reached up and opened the porthole to let in the cold wind. It blew through his hair, lifting loose strands over his eyes, and he took a deep breath.

Andrew sat quietly reading and listening to the comforting hum of the engines and the musical tinkle of a drinking glass knocking against the framed picture of his parents on the table. He finished another chapter in his book. He was becoming drowsy, the words swimming before his eyes, but a knock on his door startled him.

What could William or Claire want at this hour? Andrew asked himself, checking his watch and discovering that it was eleven thirty. He set aside the book, got up, and opened the door.

William stood outside in the hall, wearing an overcoat, and he was grinning from ear to ear. He took a step toward Andrew.

"I thought you and I could take a walk on deck, Andrew."

"It's a little late, and I was just about to turn in for the night. Maybe tomorrow." Andrew started to close the door, but William reached out and stopped it halfway. He was surprisingly strong.

"Not so fast, old boy. This is too important to wait until the morning. My sister and I have been searching everywhere for you," William said. Andrew thought about it for a second and then relented.

"Very well, give me a minute," he said, annoyed.

He stepped out into the corridor a minute later in his heavy overcoat and the cap he'd worn when he met Matthew. William motioned for Andrew to follow him.

They walked down the hall, past the elevators, and out into the vestibule of the grand staircase. Andrew and William paused on the landing and then went up the stairs, past the ornamental figures of honor and glory crowning the time: eleven thirty-four. They went out onto the boat deck and walked to a deserted stretch of deck, where they stopped and leaned over the rail, looking at the stars in the night sky and the ocean rolling past them below.

"Well, what is so important that you brought me up here to talk?" Andrew finally said.

"Did you go to *him* tonight?" William asked.

"If I did, it was because I wanted to. It appears you paid him a visit too. I want you to leave him alone, William. He's not involved in this. It's between you and me and your sister."

"I detect you have feelings for him, and I can't permit that," William said. He unbuttoned his overcoat and reached toward the inner lining.

Andrew saw a flash of silver in the light. "You don't deserve to know how I feel about Matthew, but he's better and more honorable than you or Claire, or myself for that matter."

"So noble that he's being held in an unused steerage cabin. I wonder why?" William laughed.

"You bastard!" Andrew swore.

"I only regret that I didn't get to take care of him earlier. It might have been easier. Oh well." William shrugged and stood back silently, challenging Andrew to take a swing at him.

Chapter Fifteen

As Andrew and William stood face-to-face, the sound of a distant bell clanged loudly three times, *carried to them on the wind, distracting* them. Then Andrew saw William stare wide-eyed into the darkness ahead of the ship.

"My God, look at that," William whispered.

Andrew turned and followed William's gaze. At first he didn't see anything, and then his eyes focused on it. He thought he was seeing the sails of a large whaling ship or schooner just in front of the *Titanic*, but as it came closer, he realized the massive shape ahead was an iceberg.

It looked as if the *Titanic* was going to clear it, but then Andrew heard a faint crunching sound, and the deck shuddered under his feet. Slivers of ice sparkled in the lights, and chunks fell onto the forward decks.

Matthew opened his eyes, sat up, and listened to the faint thumping sound from somewhere far away on the ship. He strained to hear it again, but there was silence. He threw aside the blanket and got out of bed, then went to the door and listened. Outside, the hall was empty.

Claire opened her eyes, listening to the faint scraping sound that woke her. Objects on her dressing table rang together and then halted. It was silent now, so she lay back in bed, but she couldn't go back to sleep.

In the smoking room, Frank Millet, William Stead, and Colonel Butt looked up from their cigars and drinks.

"What was that?" someone asked. A pale white shape drifted past the windows.

In a third-class pantry, Tom watched glassware vibrate on the bar, rims ringing musically together, and then they stopped.

Captain Smith rushed onto the bridge from his cabin, shouting, "*What was that?*"

"Iceberg, sir. I put the helm hard over to go around it and reversed the engines, but she was too close, and she hit..." the first officer explained.

Captain Smith went out and leaned over the rail to see if he could spot the berg, at the same time saying, "Close the watertight doors!"

"The doors are already closed, sir."

"Stop engines," Smith called out, followed by the ringing telegraph relaying the order to the engine room. Slowly the engines ceased their rumbling, and the *Titanic* drifted to a stop.

Andrew looked around and realized William was gone. He figured he must have gone down to his sister.

Andrew stood alone on the boat deck, watching as the iceberg drifted into the darkness behind the *Titanic*, and then gradually he noticed that the waves swept aside by the ship's forward movement slowed and stopped.

He remained outside, walking along the deck for a minute or two. Everything seemed normal, and an officer who passed him didn't look worried, so Andrew decided to return to his cabin.

When he opened the door leading to the grand staircase, he found people gathered in the landing and on the stairs looking around, curious about what had happened. Some people were dressed in evening clothes, and others wore robes and slippers. Seeing that he came from outside, a man and woman stopped him.

"Do you know what happened? Why have we stopped?" the woman said.

"We hit an iceberg, but the crew doesn't look very alarmed." Andrew smiled and went back down the stairs to his cabin. He passed other people who asked him the same question, and he gave the same response. Andrew felt important to be able to impart first-person information, having seen the iceberg scrape alongside. Though there were now people walking around and showing off chunks of ice that had fallen on board, he was the first passenger to have spotted it, except for William, who was nowhere to be seen.

Andrew didn't want to leave Matthew alone in his cabin, probably with no knowledge of what had happened. He went down the ladder to third-class and found that the way he had passed so many times before to see Matthew was locked. He shook the gate, which caught the attention of a passing sailor.

"Sir, you're not supposed to be down here. Just return to your cabin. The ship will be on its way again soon."

"My friend is down there, and I want to—" Andrew said, but he was quickly interrupted.

"Sorry, sir, not right now," the sailor said curtly, stepping close.

Andrew reluctantly backed away and turned around to go up the ladder to first class. Glancing back, he saw the sailor was still watching him.

Andrew closed his cabin door and picked up his book. He got through three paragraphs before he heard the hiss of steam being released. He raised his eyes to the framed photograph of his parents, and for a brief moment he felt his mother's apprehension about the *Titanic* being unsinkable. Again putting the book down, he opened his door and looked out into the hall. There were more people milling about, simply curious about when the ship would begin moving again.

A passing crewman saw Andrew in the doorway and told him, "Not to worry, sir. The captain is making sure the iceberg didn't scrape off too much paint. We'll be on our way in an hour or so." The man walked away and repeated the same information to another passenger farther down the hall.

Andrew closed the door and sat back down on the sofa, but after struggling through another paragraph, he gave up.

Matthew tried knocking on his door again and calling out for someone to tell him what was going on, but he got no response. He crossed the room and looked out through the small porthole. The *Titanic* wasn't moving, and steam was roaring from somewhere above him.

He sat back down on the bunk and clasped his hands over his knees. Maybe Andrew or a crewman would be down soon to tell him what in the world was going on. Nervous, he got up and went to the door again and called out.

"Hey, mates, have you forgotten me in here?" he said loudly. There was no answer.

Andrew had given up the idea of trying to read or sleep because of the voices outside his window and in the hallway, and above him the venting of steam punctured his every thought. He finally put on his heavy coat and went out into the grand staircase area. He saw Frank Millet and William Stead walking up the stairs, and he would have joined them, but once again they were too engrossed in conversation to hear Andrew when he called to them.

He was standing at the foot of the stairs when he saw Thomas Andrews coming toward him. Andrew tried to read his face, to figure out whether the news was good or bad, but Mr. Andrews's face was blank.

Andrew tried to stop him to ask, "Mr. Andrews, what's happening?"

But Thomas Andrews chose not to hear him; he passed on up the stairs. Andrew looked out of the windows facing the boat deck. People were out there, wandering about and looking around, then giving up and coming back inside where it was warmer.

Seeing that there were no further developments, Andrew went back to his cabin again, removed his coat, and threw it on the bed. He tried again to read his book. It proved fruitless, because he kept thinking about Matthew. He didn't know what was going on, but he tried to console himself with the hope that someone must have already released Matthew from the cabin. Matthew would turn up at A-17 any moment, and Andrew would tell him about seeing the iceberg. He checked his pocket watch. It was nearly midnight.

Andrew gave up on the book. Setting it aside, he picked up his pen and tried to write to his aunt and uncle. He managed to put one complete paragraph down on paper, but when he read it back to himself out loud, it made no sense. He put it aside too; he would get back to it tomorrow morning.

He paced back to the door, restless, and looked out into the hall. More people wandered about, asking questions of any steward they could find, but everyone received the same answer.

"There's nothing whatsoever to worry about. We'll be on our way again in a few hours."

Andrew shut the door.

Matthew paced the cabin nervously. The hallway remained silent, and he could still hear the roar from above him.

What's going on up there? Is there something wrong? Why has the ship stopped?

He continued to walk back and forth, glancing from time to time at the small porthole and toward the door in case he should hear some sound through either one. Matthew prayed Andrew would come, or perhaps Tom, to check on him. However, as the minutes passed, no one came.

Matthew poured a glass of water and took a drink, wishing it were whisky. He tried to make himself relax, sitting down on the bed and praying that the *Titanic* would start moving once again. He lay back on the mattress and tried to go to sleep, but the faraway sounds kept invading his dreams. He opened his eyes and stared at the door.

Chapter Sixteen

April fifteen, 1912, midnight

Captain Smith stood by himself in the chart room. Plans for the *Titanic* were laid out on the table in front of him as he waited for Thomas Andrews to assure him the damage wasn't serious. True, there was water coming in, but *Titanic* was still safe, right?

There was a knock on the door, and Captain Smith looked up as Mr. Andrews came in and stood next to him over the blueprints. He caressed them for a moment before Captain Smith spoke.

"Well? What's the verdict?" Captain Smith asked.

Mr. Andrews picked up a pencil and said, "In the first ten minutes since the collision, there's water here in the forepeak, the mailroom and cargo holds, and in boiler rooms five and six. The ship can survive the first three or four compartments breached, but not five. The weight of water in the bow will pull her down forward, and the water will spill back."

On the blueprints, Mr. Andrews tapped one watertight compartment, and the next one in line, and the next.

"The *Titanic* is going to sink."

The words sounded slow and drawn-out in Captain Smith's ears. He couldn't believe what he was hearing.

"How much time do we have?" Captain Smith remained strangely calm. He didn't want to hear the answer he received.

"An hour, perhaps longer."

"My God..." Captain Smith whispered.

Thomas Andrews again looked down at the plans of the ship he'd created and then lifted his eyes to the captain.

"The lifeboats have space for only twelve hundred people. How many are there on board?" His voice was hoarse.

"There are twenty-two hundred souls on board," Smith answered him barely above a whisper, but the room echoed with his words.

"Then there's not one second to waste," Thomas Andrews said, then left the room to take in the situation.

Captain Smith's footsteps were heavy when he went out to his officers assembled on the bridge a minute later. They stood at attention and waited.

"I never thought I would have to say this, but we have to prepare to abandon ship. Officer Murdoch, you'll muster the passengers and get them on deck. Officer Lightoller, you'll get the lifeboats uncovered, swung out, and ready to lower. I'll work out our position, give it to the wireless operators, and have them send out the call for assistance."

A knock sounded on Andrew's door.

They've released Matthew, thank God.

He rose to answer, and his steward entered as he opened the door.

"Mr. Elliot, the captain has asked all passengers to put on their life belts and go up to the boat deck. I would recommend dressing warmly," he said calmly, pulling the white, cork-filled belts from on top of the wardrobe and putting them on the bed for Andrew.

"Is it that serious, then?" Andrew asked.

"It's just to be on the safe side, sir. There's nothing to worry about," the steward said, smiling. He bowed to Andrew and then went on to the cabin next door.

Andrew put his heavy coat back on, put on one of the life belts, and tied the straps securely. He stood in the doorway and looked around, spotting the photograph of his parents next to the bed. He pulled the picture from its frame and put it in his pocket, and then he left the cabin and shut the door. An officer passed through the hallway, urging everyone to put on his or her life belt. Andrew stopped to help an elderly woman put on her belt, and then he went up toward the boat deck. On the way up, he passed William coming down, but William didn't see him. Andrew saw Mrs. Brown coming down from the boat deck with a life belt in her hand; she paused when she saw him.

"Nobody seems to know what they're doing around there, but at least there's some excitement, eh?"

"It sure looks that way. I was going to see if there's any more news," Andrew said. Mrs. Brown turned away from Andrew, and seeing some friends on the landing below, she waved and hurried down to join them.

Andrew continued up the stairs, through the crowds of people moving around him. He stood leaning over the oak banister, looking at the men and women milling about in life belts, either angry or amused at the midnight excitement. He wandered outside.

Andrew leaned against the bulkhead outside the entrance to the grand staircase, watching the sailors and officers strip the canvas covers off the lifeboats. The squeal of pulleys and cranks as the boats swung outward on their davits added to the already deafening noise. People moved impatiently around behind him, but most preferred to stay inside where it was warmer. Passing among them, he saw Captain Smith walking by, and this time Andrew stepped out in front of him.

"Captain, just how serious is the situation we're facing?" Andrew asked.

Captain Smith searched his face and then looked around him. He seemed to be deciding if he could trust Andrew or not.

Andrew stepped closer and said, "You can trust me, captain."

"The ship has only an hour to live, maybe a little more." the captain said, his voice hoarse. An officer came by and wanted to speak to the captain, and he walked away before Andrew could thank him.

Andrew was momentarily shocked. The *unsinkable Titanic* was sinking, and fast.

I have to find Matthew.

Andrew went back inside. He wanted to get below, find Matthew, and get back on deck before it was too late. He checked his pocket watch. It was 12:15 a.m.

Matthew slumped against the cabin door. He had been pounding on it since he heard someone in the hall call out, "Everyone on deck with life belts on at once!" The man had repeated the command a couple of times. Then silence.

Matthew had pounded on the door. "Hey, I'm in here. Help!" he shouted until he was almost hoarse.

He heard voices outside in the hall, and he called again. Someone did hear him, and he was sure they had stopped, because they knocked in return, but they spoke in a language he didn't understand. Whoever it was gave up and walked away. Outside the cabin, it was silent again.

Someone, a member of the crew or even Andrew, had to come soon. He turned, and a strange sight on the chest under the porthole captured his attention. The water in the glass he had set there was no longer level.

Matthew got up and threw his shoulder against the door once, then twice, and then a third time, but it wouldn't give. He tried pounding and yelling again at the top of his lungs.

"Somebody! Anybody! I'm trapped in here, get help!"

He stopped shouting and listened, but there was no one in the hall. Matthew turned around and looked at the ring of rivets around the porthole, and he thought about Daniel and his brother Ian. They had both worked on the ship, and now it had stopped in the middle of the ocean, and there was something going on outside, and everyone seemed to have forgotten he was here.

He sat back down on the bed, since there wasn't much else to do aside from pounding on the door and hoping someone could hear him.

Matthew thought about his parents and the November day he last saw them. It had been pouring rain, and the roads were knee-deep in mud. Sometime in the middle of the day, a neighbor came rushing into the house, seeking his mother.

The man's wife was going to have a baby, and the pains had started. She had to come right away. Matthew's parents grabbed their heavy coats and hurried out to the neighbor's buggy.

The last thing his mother said to him was, "We'll return soon, Matthew. There's a pot of tea on the hub, and some stew. We won't be too long."

Then the door closed. That was the last time he saw them alive. On the way back, the cart slipped in a muddy rut, the horses became frightened, and the wagon plunged into a lake.

Matthew remembered it was still pouring rain at the graveside as the minister read the service over the two coffins. He stood mostly alone, with only one or two people from the village. Ian hadn't been able to get away from his work in Belfast to attend the funeral.

When all the mourners went home, Matthew was left by himself under a soggy umbrella. He couldn't tell the difference between the water that fell from the sky and that which fell from his eyes.

The next morning, Matthew threw some clothes and his mother's rosary into a sack and made his way north to Belfast, to his brother, and eventually to Daniel.

Matthew could feel the beads in his pocket, but it had been so long since he said his prayers, he couldn't remember any of the words. He got up off the bunk and tried calling through the door once again, alternating it with pounding that might draw some attention.

The passageway outside the door was empty.

On the grand staircase, Andrew made his way through passengers going out onto the boat deck either wearing or carrying life belts. In the corner, the orchestra was gathered around the piano, playing 'Alexander's Ragtime Band'. Andrew paused briefly to listen, and then he headed down the stairs. He met Claire and William going in the opposite direction, carrying their life belts and blocking his way down the stairs.

"You two should put those belts on," Andrew said. William shrugged, and Claire reluctantly let Andrew help her put *one on* and tied the straps.

"Where are you going in such a hurry, Andrew?" Claire asked, lacing her arm through his.

"I was going down below to find someone…"

"Not right now, Andrew. There's so much going on up here," Claire insisted, looking behind Andrew toward her brother. They led a reluctant Andrew back up the stairs to the boat deck.

Andrew walked with them, quietly looking for a chance to break away among the people gathered around the deck. Above the noise, he could still hear music from behind him. Claire sat on a bench despite the bitter cold and pulled Andrew down next to her. William stood nearby; his hands jammed in his pockets.

"Claire, we shouldn't be sitting here. This is pretty serious," Andrew said, and as if to punctuate his words, there was a white flash and a pop from somewhere forward. A white streak shot skyward and burst into bright stars over the *Titanic*.

"Rockets." The word escaped the lips of everyone standing nearby. Claire frowned and pulled Andrew closer as he tried to move away.

"Claire, please, I have to…"

"Stay right here. You can't leave us at a time like this," she said. "William, will you go back and get me a scarf? It's quite cold." The wink she gave her brother wasn't lost on Andrew, and he pulled himself out of her grip. He stood up.

"Where are you going? To that *steward*?"

"His name's Matthew, and I would rather be with him than either one of you," Andrew said, preparing to walk away from them. William quickly stepped in front of him, blocking his path.

"I don't think that's a wise idea, chap."

"Stand out of my way." Andrew moved closer to him and was prepared to fight him, but an officer suddenly got between them. The man took Claire by the arm and led her toward a waiting lifeboat. She looked at Andrew and William.

"I thought I would stay around for a while," Claire said. They walked with her to the edge of the deck, and Claire looked down and then drew back. "No, I can't do this. It looks so much safer here than out in that dark ocean," she said, stepping slightly back toward Andrew and William.

"There's no time for that, Claire. Go ahead. Goodbye," Andrew said, using the opportunity to get away.

He turned and watched them over the heads of the crowd. He saw the officer help her into a lifeboat, and she paused. Claire had one foot in the boat and one on the deck, and she was saying something to William, who nodded and stepped back.

Andrew threaded his way through the crowd of people coming onto the deck and those who were waiting inside the grand staircase area, listening to the music and keeping out of the cold. He was partway down the stairs when William caught up with him.

"Thank God I caught you. It's Claire. She got away from the officer and went back to the cabin. She's refusing to leave the safety of the ship for a dark night in a rowboat."

"I didn't see her pass me on the way down," Andrew said.

"There are too many people about, so of course you didn't see her. Now come on, let's hurry. They won't hold the boat forever," William insisted.

"All right, let's make this quick," Andrew said, following William down to their cabin.

William opened the door, and Andrew rushed past him into the room, calling out, "Claire, this is ridiculous, you have to get in a lifeboat…" Andrew found the room was empty, and when he turned around, William had a gun pointed at him.

"Clever ruse, eh? She's probably safely away from the ship by now."

"This ship is sinking. I *must get to* Matthew before it's too late." Andrew took a step around him toward the door, but William raised his pistol and got in his way.

"One false move, old chap, and my sister will be a widow before she's married. Matthew, well, he'll go down with the ship, trapped in his little cube. Too damned bad he didn't force you to stay away when I threatened him."

"He told me you came to see him. You had no right."

"I'm the brother of your fiancée. I have every right." William laughed as if it were a joke.

"You keep reminding me of that, but I won't marry her. I want to be with *him*, and that's all you need to know," Andrew said.

"Yes, you keep saying that, but yet you and I are up here on the upper decks of a sinking ship while your little steward is shut up somewhere below. You'll never make it down there and back, so forget about him."

"Never. Not if he needs me. I have to try."

"It may well be too late. I may have already killed him since you saw him last."

William laughed, and Andrew felt heat rising to his face. He stepped toward William, who moved backward. There was a knock on the door, and someone on the other side called out.

"Is anybody in there?"

"We're getting some things together. We'll be along in a minute or two!" William shouted. He then turned his attention back to Andrew.

"If you hurt him, I'll get that gun and shoot you myself!"

"Go ahead, old man. I know you want to." William raised his hands in the air, letting the pistol dangle by the trigger guard, taunting Andrew to grab it.

Andrew lunged forward, landing on top of William, and knocking him backward on the carpet. The gun fell out of his hand. They wrestled, William's punches missing Andrew, who was quicker. Finally, William was able to move, and this time he pinned Andrew down with the weight of his body. He reached for his gun.

"You should have taken this while you had the chance. Now get up," William ordered.

"What's your plan now?" Andrew inquired, scanning the room for something he could use as a weapon. There was nothing. "You won't get away with this, William, you or your sister, if she is really your sister. Getting yourself invited into the homes of the wealthy, living off them in comfort, and stealing from them," Andrew said, remaining calm.

"I knew there was a smart man hiding behind the bookish, chess playing, dreaming poof. Claire is my wife, and we invented the whole *orphaned-brother-and-sister* act when we performed in the theater together. If we hadn't, we would be living in a single room somewhere in London cooking rats for dinner. As the poor children of a defunct gentleman, people felt sorry for us. Wealthy people like your family ate out of our hands. They showered us with trips, clothes, jewels, and money. We bet that nobody from the upper classes would have seen our performances, and we were right... *though that woman we met the first night in the dining saloon almost gave us away, damnable luck, she walked away without pressing the matter further, which might have made things bad for us but nobody's perfect.*" William grinned, then laughed.

Andrew looked from the design in the carpet and up at William. "Where did I figure in all of this?"

"When we came to your house over the holidays, your father was desperate to get his poof of a son married as soon as possible to avoid prison or scandal.

Claire and I decided it was the perfect opportunity, especially when he offered to pay our expenses to America to keep an eye on you until any possible talk died down. Relax. My darling wife pawned a bracelet for our passage money. We didn't want to appear too desperate. It would have been the perfect arrangement. We could live in relative comfort, and you could do whatever... Of course, we didn't figure on you meeting *someone on the boat.* We had to do something."

"When we're rescued, I'll see you both get prison for this," Andrew threatened, but William looked scornful.

"You should thank me for doing you a favor, Mr. Elliot. Too bad, with him locked up in steerage and you up here, you won't get to die together, and the truth about Claire and myself you'll take to the ocean floor with you."

William started laughing again, and Andrew sprang at him, knocking him to the floor. The gun fell from William's hand and clattered under the bed, out of reach as he and William struggled, rising to their feet.

Just when Andrew thought he had an advantage in the fight, William pushed him back, and Andrew fell and hit his head on *the corner of the* open trunk behind him. He sagged to the floor.

Matthew strained his neck to look out the porthole. Above him there was a bright flash and a popping hiss that died away. He heard distant noises from the decks, and out on the water, he saw a lifeboat bathed in the ship's lights, rowing away. Another one, oars extended, was just pulling away from the side. He went back to the door and alternately shouted and pounded, but he gave up after a few minutes, because he received no reply.

He sat on the bunk, his fists tightly squeezing the mattress as he fought off panic.

Chapter Seventeen

Monday, April fifteen, 1912, one a.m.

Captain Smith stood back and watched as another white distress rocket shot into the sky and burst into a shower of sparks above the *Titanic*. A light shone on the horizon—not a star, but definitely a ship. Still, the rockets and the wireless operators failed to contact it. They did reach another ship, the *Carpathia*, which was making speed to come to *Titanic*'s aid. Four hours, her operator had informed them earlier. Captain Smith prayed it would be sooner. The water was lapping at the name *Titanic* on the bow.

Andrew opened his eyes and sat up. His head ached, and the overpowering smell of flowers assaulted his senses; a bottle of perfume had fallen over, and its contents spilled across the table and onto the carpet. He pulled himself onto the bed and sat there until the wave of nausea passed and he could finally stand up.

Now that he could think clearly, his first thought was to get to Matthew; he prayed there would be time to be angry and go after William later. He tried the door, and it was locked. He took several steps back and then rushed at the door with his shoulder, but it wouldn't move. He tried it again, and still the wood wouldn't give. There was a connecting door leading to the next cabin, but it too was locked. Andrew tried rushing at that also, but with the same result; it wouldn't budge.

The gun I knocked out of William's hand. Andrew looked under the bed where he recalled it had fallen, but found it gone. He went back to the door and started pounding, calling out at the top of his lungs.

"Hey! Hello! Is anyone out there? I'm locked in!" Andrew shouted a couple of times but received no response. He stepped back, and then he had an idea. *Maybe I can pry open the lock?* He searched the room for something with which to pick the lock, and on the table among combs and brushes and the jewelry box, he found a jeweled silver letter opener.

It took several minutes of trying different methods, but at last he heard a click, and the door opened. But as it did so, the letter opener broke, and it was now useless. Andrew dropped the pieces on the floor and hurried out to reach Matthew. Halfway down the corridor, a steward stopped him and instructed him to get to the boat deck. Andrew shook his head.

"I can't leave this ship until I get to Matthew," Andrew told him. The steward shrugged and walked away. Andrew pulled out his pocket watch. It was one-fifteen a.m.

"I'm sorry, sir. You can't go down this way." The sailor blocked Andrew's way down the ladder.

"I've gone down this ladder to visit my friend several times, and nobody stopped me."

"That may be, sir, but not tonight." He folded his arms in front of Andrew and refused to move, and another crewman came and stood next to the first, also refusing to budge. Andrew looked behind him at several passengers with children and luggage being held back behind the gate.

"Let those people up to the lifeboats. We're in the middle of a real emergency here. You can't do this," Andrew pleaded, but the men wouldn't move, and when he tried moving one of the sailors aside, he was roughly shoved back for his efforts.

Andrew gave up and went back. He knew of one other way to reach Matthew, but he had hesitated about going that way because he didn't know how much time the *Titanic* had left. He had gone that route with the steward who'd brought the dinner to Matthew's cabin earlier. He would have to go down to D-Deck, through the dining room, through the kitchens, into second class, and down one more deck. Andrew had no choice but to take that way, regardless of how much time was left.

He hurried back to the grand staircase and found the elevators around the corner out of service. He took the steps, jumping them two at a time, past abandoned clothing and blankets, weaving through people who were on their way up.

Andrew paused at the foot of the grand staircase on D-Deck, looking around the empty reception room. A loud, creaking groan made by the settling ship temporarily muffled the cheerful music of the orchestra and the sounds of people from the upper decks. Two men and a woman carrying a leather suitcase ran past him up the stairs, their footsteps fading away. The *Titanic* groaned loudly, and from somewhere the crash of glass breaking rang out. There was water gushing up the stairs from the deck below, and the Oriental carpet on the landing began to float on the greenish surface.

He hurried through the reception room and the doors of the dining room, then ran past the tables, which had been set for breakfast, and into the kitchen.

Two men in white jackets were busy removing loaves of bread from racks and placing them into a canvas bag; they stopped when they saw Andrew. Neither man questioned his presence in a crew-only domain.

Andrew only heard a scrap of their conversation as he came near. "Bread for the lifeboats…" one of them said to the other.

Andrew didn't hear the rest as he hurried past them to the doors at the far end. He ran through the empty food preparation areas and pantries to the second-class dining room. The groaning, gurgling noises the *Titanic* was making as it sank were growing louder, and the lights dimmed, leaving Andrew in the dark for a second before they came back on. He moved without stopping, down one deck and through a hallway to a flight of stairs where a gate to third-class was open and unguarded. He went down and saw only a handful of people rushing around, but they paid him no attention.

Matthew was sitting on the bunk after another unsuccessful attempt to get someone to open the door and let him out. He was covered in sweat, and his voice was scratchy from shouting. His glass had fallen off the cabinet and broken, and when he cupped his hands under the faucet to get water, there was only a meager trickle.

"Hey, is anybody out there? Send help... I'm trapped in here!" he yelled again, and still there was no response.

"I might as well face it. Nobody can hear me..." Matthew dropped back onto the bunk. His regret was that the ship would sink, and he'd never see Andrew again.

He put his head in his hands, and he almost didn't hear the pounding on the door until he recognized a familiar voice.

"Matthew... Matthew, it's me, Andrew!"

"Thank, God. I thought you would never come!" Matthew called from his side of the door.

"I won't leave you. I'm going to get you out of there. Hang on awhile longer!" Andrew said. He looked around the hall but saw nothing he could use as a battering ram. He tried his shoulder against the door a couple of times.

"I tried that, and it won't give," Matthew said.

"I'll have to find another way," Andrew said.

"Just leave me, Andrew, and save yourself. There can't be much time," Matthew responded from his side, sounding slightly panicked.

"Nonsense. I'm not leaving this ship without you," Andrew said, leaning against the opposite wall and trying to think of a solution. He wished the letter opener he had used to free himself hadn't broken, but it was too late to fret over it. Then he remembered seeing some firefighting equipment in the kitchens. He went up to the door and yelled to Matthew, "I'll be right back. I may have a solution."

"I'll be waiting right here…" Matthew laughed nervously over the exchange. "There's nowhere I can run, is there?" he said to himself. Andrew turned the corner and was on the stairs going up when he stopped. The gate that had been open just minutes before was now closed, and when he tried it, he found it was locked.

"Hey, is anybody there? The gate's locked!" he shouted, but only heard silence. He pounded at the gate once more, and it rattled but didn't budge. He wrapped both hands around the bars and bowed his head against one of his hands.

An ominous groan came from the ship, and then a loud crack, as if something was being pulled apart. The lights dimmed.

Andrew pressed his eyes shut. "This is it. She's going down…" he said between gritted teeth, but then the noise suddenly stopped, and the lights became bright again. Andrew straightened up. If it was the end, he wanted to be with Matthew. He turned and went back down.

He stood in front of the door, dreading to tell Matthew the news. "Matthew, it's me…"

"Thank God it's you, Andrew. Did you bring something to get me out of here?"

Andrew knew his pause gave Matthew the *dreaded* answer. "Don't worry, there's got to be a solution, and I'll find it."

"Then forget about me, Andrew. Get out of here and save yourself before it's too late."

"I'm not going anywhere until I have you out of there and we can leave together," Andrew said. He thought he heard a sob from the other side. "We're not defeated yet, Matthew. There must be something…"

Andrew stepped back and returned to the stairs. The gate was still closed. He went back to Matthew.

"Matthew, do you know if there's a pantry or some kind of a crew ladder around?" he shouted.

Matthew replied after a pause. "I don't know where the crew's ladder is from here, but there's a pantry. You should have passed it on your way here; it's around the corner. What good is a pantry going to do? Don't tell me you're hungry," Matthew said.

"No, but I have an idea, and if I find what I'm looking for, it might work. Matthew, I have to leave you for a minute, but I want you to know…"

"I know, Andrew. I feel the same way too," Matthew said.

Andrew felt cheered by his words. He paused, and then said, "Just sit tight and think about going toTexas. I'll be back soon."

Around the corner, he found a door with a sign that read Pantry. He tried the door and it swung open. Andrew rummaged the drawers and cupboards. He found plates and spoons and butter knives that weren't as sharp as a letter opener, and things to make coffee and tea, but there was nothing useful for his purpose. Just then the door swung closed, pushed by a metal coatrack that suddenly crashed to the floor. Andrew looked at it for a second and then had an idea.

He returned, holding the metal rod from the coatrack in front of him. "Matthew, stand back."

"What are you going to do?"

"Just stand back," Andrew said. He moved several paces back, and then ran at the door with his makeshift ram. There was a loud thud as he heaved against it, and then three more times. Finally, on the fifth try, he saw the wood between the door and the frame split. He took another run at it, and at last the lock shattered and the door swung open. Andrew dropped his battering ram, and a second later he and Matthew were in each other's arms, kissing and nearly crying with relief.

"I told you I would get you out of here somehow," Andrew said as they once again kissed and held on to each other.

"It would be nice to hold onto you for a while longer, but we have to move," Andrew said, urgently.

Chapter Eighteen

A wave of foaming green seawater swept around the cranes, hatches, and the base of the mast as the bow dipped under the ocean. A white streak shot upward, and the sparks lit up the scene for those rowing away in the lifeboats. Then the sparks faded, leaving everything dark again.

The people in the lifeboats stared in disbelief. The *Titanic* was still brightly lit up, even though the rows of portholes angled down into the ocean, and across the water they could hear the orchestra playing a waltz. It still looked so safe and warm. They couldn't believe they were sitting in rowboats in the dark, watching silently as events slowly unfolded in front of them.

"Put this on, Matthew, and let's get out of here while there's time," Andrew said as he removed the life belt and heavy topcoat and put the coat and belt on Matthew. The coat was too long, and it nearly dragged on the floor as Matthew moved about. Andrew couldn't help but chuckle.

"It feels like I'm wearing a dress, mate." Matthew laughed.

"I'm afraid the tailor is out rowing tonight," Andrew said. The lights dimmed and came back on. They stood for a second, looking at each other.

"We better move. I think she may go at any minute," Andrew said, taking Matthew by the hand and leading him to the staircase. The gate was still locked, and Andrew looked at Matthew.

"I'm sorry, but they took my keys when they…"

Andrew stepped away and came back a moment later with the rack he had broken Matthew out with. Together they charged up the stairs toward the locked grating, then again. It rattled, but nothing happened. They gave it a few more tries, but the lock held fast. Matthew cursed loudly.

Andrew and Matthew walked through a maze of passages until they came to a partly open door, which Matthew recognized.

"This leads to the crew quarters and Scotland Road…"

"What's that?" Andrew questioned as they stepped over the doorway.

"It's a service corridor that runs the full length of the ship. There's an entrance into first class at the other end."

They ran down the hallway, and then stopped, finding themselves suddenly ankle-deep in water that was soon up to their knees. Even as they backed up to go in the other direction, a geyser of water began to pour around the edges of a door. Andrew and Matthew turned and ran, the water rising fast behind them, forcing them back the way they had come.

"Never mind, we'll find another way up." Andrew was confident as they moved down the passageway, trying unmarked doors that might conceal a ladder, until at last they found an open hatch with a ladder that led downward toward the engine room. They exchanged a glance, and Matthew was the first to speak what they were both thinking.

"It looks like we may have to go downward to find our way up," Matthew said.

Andrew felt slightly doubtful, but he knew Matthew might be right. He motioned to the ladder. "After you, sir," he said, making Matthew laugh.

"So polite…" Matthew smiled as he descended the ladder. Andrew followed.

At the bottom of the ladder, they found themselves in a large open space leading to a passage and more doors. Matthew opened one of the doors and found refrigerated meat suspended from hooks; behind another door, he found fresh fruit.

They paused, staring at each other.

"Come on, Matthew, there are more doors, so let's try them all. There has to be a ladder behind one of them," Andrew said as he threw open another and found bottled spirits. Matthew looked doubtful.

"We'll make it, Matthew, with plenty of time to spare," Andrew encouraged, trying to cheer him up.

It was Matthew who found the ladder down a short passage behind a partly open metal hatch. Andrew joined him at the bottom of the ladder and looked up.

They shared a quick hug before they scrambled up the stairs.

"Where are we?" Matthew asked as he and Andrew surveyed the place where the stairs ended.

"We have no choice but to find out. Let's try this way," Andrew said, leading Matthew around a corner. They came to an open door and went through it. Andrew recognized the room immediately.

"The second-class dining saloon..." Andrew said with some relief. He recalled a staircase leading up just outside the room. Andrew started for the door, but paused because Matthew had hung behind. He went back.

"Come on, Matthew, we can do this. This is second class, and there're stairs outside the room that *have* to lead up to the boat deck."

"Andrew, if we don't make it up there and the ship sinks, I want you to know that I—"

"Don't say that. That's no way to talk. We're going to make it up in time, and you know I feel the same way about you. I came after you, didn't I?"

"You must think I'm such a fool, huh? Arrested, and now I'm afraid we're going to die on a sinking ship." Matthew laughed bitterly.

Andrew drew closer, put his arm around him, and pulled Matthew near *to him*. "What kind of a way is that to talk? We're not going to die, Matthew, and whatever may have happened in your past or mine doesn't matter. We have to look forward," Andrew said, trying to smile.

Matthew looked up at him, and his lips lifted in a trace of a grin.

"Let's go." Andrew led Matthew out of the dining saloon and up the stairs, and at last the door opened out onto the boat deck. The bitter cold air hit them immediately. Matthew tried to give back the coat, but Andrew waved it away.

"I'm fine. Let's keep moving," Andrew said.

There was a crowd around the remaining lifeboats, so Andrew and Matthew walked through them toward the front of the ship and entered through the entrance of the grand staircase, past the orchestra, and down the stairs. Halfway down, they paused to look over the banister at the dark green seawater creeping closer to them. The lights had dimmed, and were beginning to burn with a dull, red glow.

Andrew led Matthew to his cabin to fetch his extra overcoat. He removed a coat from the wardrobe and put it on. Then he took down the extra life belt and put it on over the coat. "There, now let's get out of here," Andrew said.

They were sharing *a quick* embrace when suddenly the door swung open. A crewman poked his head into the room. "Gentlemen, you'd better hurry. There's not much time," he said, breathless, and then hurried away.

Andrew and Matthew remained a second longer before they stepped out into the hall.

"Let's see if there're any boats left," Andrew said, leading Matthew toward the grand staircase. There was a large crowd of people running up and down the stairs, and Andrew led Matthew to one side of the wrought banister to let them pass by.

Andrew and Matthew were just turning to go up the staircase to the boat deck when they looked up and saw William among the crowd on the landing. William turned around and saw them.

William started elbowing people out of the way to reach them. They went down the stairs to the deck below, splashing through cold water that was up to their knees. Andrew tripped; his legs tangled in a carpet floating loosely just under the surface of the water. Matthew stopped to help him up, and they held on to each other until they saw William coming around the corner. Andrew and Matthew leapt over a potted palm that had fallen from its stand. They ran up the tilting corridor.

"There's another staircase that leads to the promenade deck, just up this way," Andrew explained as they ran up the slanting deck, with William following, though he lagged behind, slowed by the slope of the floor and the people still hurrying about.

Andrew and Matthew reached the staircase and hurried up the steps, stumbling once or twice. At last, they reached the main foyer, and had to jump out of the way as a cart of silverware and dishes rolled toward them, crashing and clattering around their feet. Looking back, Andrew didn't see William anywhere behind them. The lights dimmed again, leaving everything in the dark, and then they flickered back on long enough for Andrew and Matthew to reach the revolving door to the smoking room across from where they stood.

They ran together through the room, but Andrew stopped. Frank Millet, William Stead, and Colonel Archie Butt were seated at a table, chatting quietly. The chess pieces in front of Frank Millet had fallen and scattered, and he looked up and smiled at Andrew.

"It looks like our game of chess has been temporarily delayed, my boy."

"Won't you try to save yourselves?" Andrew asked.

William Stead picked up a book and started reading, and Archie Butt shook his head. Frank Millet looked thoughtful for a minute, and then he said, "There's plenty of time yet, my boy, but you'd better go. Good luck to you both."

"Good luck to you, sir." Andrew shook his hand.

Matthew gently touched Andrew's shoulder. "Come on, Andrew, we have to hurry." Andrew nodded at his friends once more and then followed Matthew to the door leading to the verandah café. He let Matthew go ahead, and he paused to smile faintly at Thomas Andrews, who stood leaning against the fireplace, his life belt discarded on a table nearby. Mr. Andrews didn't even seem to notice him. Looking behind, Andrew saw William pushing through the revolving doors. He ran to join Matthew, who was waiting for him.

Andrew and Matthew found themselves *amid* a mob of people pushing and shoving back toward the stern of the *Titanic*, which was rising higher out of the ocean. Matthew lost his hold on Andrew's hand and discovered that the panicking crowd had pushed them apart and pinned Andrew against a railing. Matthew fought his way to Andrew's side.

"This doesn't look too good, does it?" Andrew said when Matthew finally reached him.

"We'll have to try another way. Come on." Matthew pulled him out of the way. There was no way to run except for a ladder that led upward to the boat deck. Andrew went up and jumped over the railing, and Matthew followed.

"Where do we go now?" Matthew asked. Andrew looked around him. It was becoming difficult to see in the fading reddish glow of the lights. They stood together on the tilting deck while people pushed and shoved around them. Someone on the edge of the deck *jumped* overboard, and another man ran in front of them, carrying a deck chair that he threw into the ocean. Nearby, gathered in a corner, a group of men and women were kneeling around a minister, their hands raised in prayer, ignoring the panic around them.

They pushed through the crowd to the edge of the deck, between two empty lifeboat davits, and looked down at the dark water below them, then at each other. In front of them hung the empty ropes from the lifeboat davits, inviting them to reach out and lower themselves down to the water. A man shoved them out of the way, grabbing the ropes. They watched him let go halfway down; Matthew didn't see him again.

"It's too far to jump from here. Let's go this way... Trust me," Andrew said, clutching Matthew's hands.

Together they ran forward. Getting closer, Matthew saw a group of men struggling to release one of the collapsible lifeboats from the roof over the bridge.

Andrew and Matthew joined the men pushing the boat to the edge of the roof, where boards had been set to guide it to the deck. It landed right side up on the deck. There was too much noise, but Matthew could hear all sorts of commands being given by a man in an officer's coat and cap. The lifeboat davits were cranked back, and block and tackle attached to them, but it was clear there might not be any time.

Matthew saw a wall of water rising upward and spilling around their feet. Someone shouted, "Give me a knife, cut the ropes..."

Music was still coming from somewhere nearby, and Matthew recognized the hymn 'Nearer, My God To Thee'. Mesmerized, both he and Andrew stopped to listen, but then the music couldn't be heard over a series of sounds that were like gunfire. Matthew pushed Andrew out of the way as one of the cables supporting the first funnel snapped and missed them by mere inches. The funnel's base crumpled like a tin can and fell over, striking the water. It barely missed the lifeboat that had drifted off the deck with a handful of people clinging to it. *Andrew and Matthew pushed through the crowd, separated briefly they found each other a few feet away.*

The swirling foam of dark water was washing toward them; there wouldn't be any time to reach the stern. They would have to jump for it. The water was swirling around their knees. Moving back, away from the rising water, Andrew pulled Matthew toward the edge of the boat deck. He had one arm around Matthew's waist and another clinging to a rope that dangled from an empty lifeboat davit. They both looked down the short distance to the dark water.

"We have to do this, Matthew. It's now or never," Andrew said before his voice was lost in a rumbling earthquake sound as china, furniture, and countless loose objects inside the ship shifted and fell.

"Come on, jump and I'll follow you!" Andrew shouted above the roaring noise that was coming from all around them.

Matthew held on to Andrew's hand for a brief second, squeezing, and they looked into each other's eyes, giving silent encouragement. Then Matthew jumped. The water was bitterly cold, and when he surfaced, he could barely breathe. That he had to find Andrew was his only thought. The ship towered above him in the darkness. People were jumping, splashing near him, crying out as they fell into the water.

Matthew looked around him, but he couldn't see Andrew in the faces of the people swimming past him.

He was sure Andrew had jumped; Andrew had said he would follow him.

He called out. "Andrew... Andrew, do you hear me!"

No response.

Matthew looked behind him at the ship. The rudder and propellers were outlined against the stars. Just then the lights blinked once, came on again with a bright flash, and then went dark. Matthew had never swum so fast in his life; even the bitter cold water didn't bother him. His first thought had been to find Andrew, and the second was to get as far away from the *Titanic* as possible. He thought he heard someone calling his name several times, but too much was happening, and he couldn't locate the voice in the dark, ***now mingled with a chorus of many voices***

Matthew saw an object in the water just ahead of him, and he swam toward it. It was a suitcase, and he used it as a paddle to kick away from the sinking ship behind him, but he only got a few feet. Suddenly he felt an arm wrapping around his neck and pulling him away from his makeshift life-ring. They struggled in the water over the case, punching and kicking, until finally the stranger and the suitcase sank from sight.

Behind him he heard an explosive pop, and then wood and metal showered him from above. Matthew turned around and saw the *Titanic* breaking in half. Sparks and debris shot skyward, the remaining two funnels toppled over, and what was left of the forward section began to sink, pulling the stern upright. It hung like a giant black shape pointing up at the sky, and he could see it outlined against the stars.

Then slowly the *Titanic* began moving, water flooding in faster and pulling it down until the ocean closed over the flagstaff at the very tail of the ship, leaving an eruption of water in its wake. The *Titanic* was gone.

Chapter Nineteen

Monday, April fifteen, 1912, two-forty-five a.m.

Andrew was cold and his fingers numb, but he still scanned the water, looking for Matthew. The cries of the people in the water were growing fainter, and the number of people thrashing near the boat began to thin out. Occasionally the boat, which was riding low in the water, would rock violently as someone tried to climb in, but it was too dark for Andrew to discern whether they had been successful or not.

He wanted to sleep, but he was afraid to close his eyes, as he might miss rescuing Matthew from the water.

Andrew was aware that someone was sitting next to him, and he turned to see who it was. His voice was hoarse when he whispered, "Matthew... is that you?"

"I'm not Matthew... I don't know who you're talking about."

The response was from a voice that sounded familiar, but Andrew couldn't place it. Andrew lowered his head in disappointment. He and Matthew had come through the sinking, only to be separated.

Andrew shivered, and the unseen figure next to him huddled closer. Andrew didn't try to move away. He sat motionless, looking out over the dark water, praying Matthew would somehow appear. Once, he thought he saw him in the water, but when he found strength to reach out to him, it was only a patch of cork bobbing among pieces of debris.

The water was up to his ankles, but Matthew was so preoccupied thinking about Andrew that he didn't notice the cold as he stood with the other men on the bottom of one of the two lifeboats that had floated off the sinking ship. This one was now floating upside down.

He'd jumped only seconds before Andrew, but a wave had separated them before Andrew reached the water. Matthew thought he saw him, and he'd called Andrew's name several times, but he doubted Andrew could hear over the uproar. He swam toward where he thought Andrew was, but the harder he paddled, the farther away he seemed to be from him. After the *Titanic* sank, he swam about searching for Andrew until exhaustion had begun to set in and claim him as another victim. Just then he'd bumped against something solid, an overturned boat with two passengers and an officer standing on it. They helped him aboard, and now there were twenty men balanced on it, clinging to each other, praying and struggling to keep from falling into the water.

Matthew squinted into the darkness at the faces around him, hoping one of them might be Andrew, but he wasn't there. Eventually his mind became too numb to think and his legs too weak to balance on the bottom of the lifeboat any longer. He thought about how easy it would be for him to fall asleep, slip overboard, and vanish like others who had climbed on the boat after the sinking. Exhaustion overcame them, and then there was one less man on board.

Gradually he felt his eyes growing heavy, and his knees buckled, but just then someone pushed him awake. A voice growled in his ear, "Don't fall asleep, boy. Keep your eyes open for me."

"But I'm so cold and tired. Just let me shut my eyes for a minute," Matthew protested like a child. Again, an elbow dug into his back.

"I know you are, but if you want to live to see the daylight and the people you love, don't go to sleep," the voice whispered. Matthew lifted his head and blinked several times. He wanted to turn around and face the man who was speaking to him.

"Don't look back or you'll fall... Tell me about the one you love," the man said.

"Andrew is the handsomest man I've ever seen. He rescued me, and I *couldn't* rescue him," Matthew said, then suddenly realized he'd just admitted to a perfect stranger that he loved a man.

He expected to be shoved into the water, but instead the man whispered hoarsely into his ear, "You can't be sure he's gone, boy. He could be on a lifeboat thinking about you this very minute, eh?"

"I wish I shared your confidence. I was lucky to find this boat in the dark…"

"We were all blessed to find it, boy, but we'll be rescued soon. One of the wireless officers survived, and he says that the *Carpathia* should be here soon," the man whispered.

Matthew felt cheered only slightly that a ship was on its way.

There was silence again, but Matthew noticed it was becoming lighter, and then he saw a faint light on the distant horizon.

"Look. Is that a star or the rescue ship?" Matthew asked over his shoulder. No answer.

Other men on the boat saw the light too, and the officer in charge said loudly, so everyone could hear, "Keep the boat trim, stay calm!" Everyone obeyed, trying to stand still.

Then Matthew saw someone pointing. The man said, "Look over there. It's a lifeboat." Matthew squinted hard into the dim light, and he saw it too. It wasn't close, but it was a lifeboat, and it was rowing in their direction. The officer reached into his pocket, and the blasts of his whistle shattered the quiet. There was an answering shout, and the boat began rowing toward them.

The process of transfer from the overturned boat was slow, but at last Matthew was helped on board, and a blanket was placed over his shoulders. The sky was somewhat light, and he could make out the details of some of the faces around him, but the only face he was hoping and wanting to see wasn't there. He lowered his head.

Andrew felt his mind start to drift from the struggle to remain awake and the urgent need to sleep. He remembered his mother's anxiety over the voyage, and his own began to return, and his imagination began to run wild. He saw Robert standing in the door of a barn, with his arms reaching out to him, and Andrew was tempted to go to him, but his feet wouldn't work. He saw William and Claire laughing at him and pointing, and then Matthew was smiling and encouraging him to hang on.

"Aye, mate, you can make it out of this. Hold on a wee bit longer for me."

"Matthew... are you alive? Is that you?" Andrew's voice was hoarse. The vision of Matthew didn't speak, and then he was gone.

It began to grow lighter, and Andrew could make out lifeboats and drifting ice. He turned his head with some effort and looked behind him. A man was seated with his head on his chest, looking as if he was asleep, but Andrew knew different. Someone sat to his left, the one whose voice sounded familiar, and Andrew squinted into his face. The man noticed Andrew looking at him, and he managed a smile, whispering hoarsely, "Yes, old chap. I see we both made it."

"I can't say I'm glad to hear that," Andrew said.

"I always win at everything, Andrew Elliot, and I couldn't disappoint my dear Claire by going down with the ship."

"I'm too exhausted to argue with you, and if I still had the gun…"

"Ha, still pining away for that steward. What did you say his name was? Matthew?"

"You know very well what his name is."

"Now that he's out of the picture, you and Claire can be married," William said. Andrew looked away and cast his eyes toward the water. He wished he had the strength to throw himself off the boat and into the ocean, but he couldn't get his body to obey his brain. William reached out a hand, touching his shoulder.

"I can't let you do that, old man. I may have to rethink my plans for you, Mr. Elliot, and it won't be easy," William chuckled. Andrew shrugged off his grip.

"You can go to bloody hell, Mr. Bennett," Andrew said with surprising strength between chattering teeth. He could feel William moving closer to him.

Andrew remained silent. He didn't want to say anything more, even though William tried to engage him in conversation. He ignored William, and then Andrew saw a faint light glowing on the horizon. A flash rose just above the light.

"Look, a rocket," he said, pointing to the southern horizon. It was at the same time that their half-submerged boat was spotted by another lifeboat rowing by.

Someone sitting in the boat near Andrew waved his arms and called out, "Help, we're over here!"

Ten minutes later, Andrew and the others had been taken on board. Andrew tried to help row, but he was too tired to pull the oar, and a sailor gently took it away before giving him a blanket.

Matthew didn't see the rockets, but he heard commotion in the boat and saw somebody pointing at something. He lifted his body and turned to look. He was just in time to see another signal from the ship burst in the sky. He had never been happier to see anything in his life.

Pulling the blanket, he had been given tighter around his body, Matthew felt hot tears on his face despite the cold, tears for Andrew, who couldn't share this moment with him. He sat back, hugging the blanket even tighter around himself, and watched as the ship drew closer. The long night was finally over.

Chapter Twenty

Monday, April fifteen, 1912, eight a.m.

Andrew climbed the rope ladder when his turn came, because the canvas cargo net was for children and the injured. Except for missing Matthew and being tired and cold, he felt fine. When he stepped through the hatch of the rescue ship *Carpathia,* a steward bombarded him with questions.

"Name... what class are you? Are you in need of medical assistance?" the man asked.

"Andrew Elliot... first class, and I'm just tired and hungry," Andrew answered him mechanically. Before he could explain that he was searching for someone, he was being ushered to another crewman stationed in a passage a few feet away.

"First class is this way. You'll find hot coffee, brandy, and food in the first-class dining room," he told Andrew.

Andrew walked past a line of *Titanic* passengers standing in the hallway, looking for missing family and friends. He felt them searching his face and looking quickly away. He walked into the dining room, where a mug of coffee was pressed into his cold hands; he didn't even feel the heat from the heavy porcelain.

Matthew was only slightly aware that he was being lifted up the side of the ship in the canvas bag. When his turn to climb the rope ladder had come, and just as he lifted one foot to the wooden slat, he suddenly became weak. If *Titanic*'s second officer, Charles Lightoller, hadn't been standing behind him, he would have fallen into the ocean.

Matthew's vision became blurry. He thought he saw hands reaching out to pull him aboard, and he felt someone's strong arms lift him onto a hard surface, perhaps a table. Other hands undressed him and wrapped him in blankets; brandy was passed over his lips from a metallic spoon, and burned his throat.

A man held up the overcoat—Andrew's overcoat. *Andrew.*

"His name is Andrew Elliot. It's in the lining of the coat. There's a photograph of a man and woman in the right side pocket, water- damaged," he heard a voice say while a pencil scratched. He used his remaining strength to grab at whoever was standing there.

"No... I'm Matthew," he croaked. A man with a cap bent over him, pressing him back down onto the table. He insisted again. "I'm Matthew..."

"Relax, son, you can talk to us later. In the meantime, I'm going to hang this next to the bake stove to dry with the rest of your clothes," the man told him, and then he walked away and left Matthew on the table, his fuzzy vision focusing on the ceiling. He heard voices all around him, but he couldn't understand what was being said. The faces of men and women looked intently at him, and they all became Andrew's face. Feebly he tried to lift his head.

"Andrew, is that you?" he asked, and then the faces went away. Matthew felt his body, especially his feet, tingling, and under all the blankets, he was shivering.

Two others came to examine him. "He'll live. The warmth will return to his body soon…"

Matthew didn't hear any more as he fell fast asleep.

Andrew was standing in the doorway of the cabin in his dress clothes, leaning on the doorframe, smiling at him. Matthew was sitting on the metal bunk in the cramped cabin, looking back at him. The walls, the tiled floor, and the blankets on the beds seemed unusually bright, and Matthew had to shield his eyes. Andrew was still in the same position.

"Was it all a dream, Andrew? The Titanic didn't go down, and you're here in the morning like you promised?" Matthew looked beyond Andrew to see if the steward was bringing breakfast.

Andrew ceased smiling and looked down at the red-tiled floor and then back up at Matthew.

"I wish I could tell you it was a dream, but it wasn't. But you survived, and that means you have the chance to start over. No more Lord Carson seeking to have you arrested. You don't even have to think about Daniel. You're not a prisoner in this cabin any longer. You're free to head west like you want…"

"Not without you," Matthew protested. How did Andrew know about Daniel? He couldn't recall talking about him.

"Why not without me?"

"I lost you in the ocean. I saw you, and then I didn't, and the water was so cold."

"You don't know that you lost me. So many things happened after we hit the water," Andrew said.

"I never got to tell you how much I love you."

"I know, but you'll have plenty of chances for that. Plenty of chances…"

Matthew opened his eyes. He felt warmer than he had before, and he was still looking up at the same plain white ceiling. He had been moved from the table to a mattress on the floor a few feet away. He was also aware that a lot of people were around him. Some quietly sobbed, and others sat on the floor or stood in groups talking. A man with a black moustache was sitting at his feet, wrapped in a blanket. Matthew sat up on his elbows, drawing the attention of the man who sat next to him.

"It wasn't a nightmare?" Matthew said to him.

"The greatest ship ever built hits an iceberg and is gone just like that." He snapped his fingers.

Matthew lay back on the mattress in shock. *The unsinkable ship is gone? I didn't imagine the whole thing.* "It doesn't seem possible… Was everyone saved?" Matthew finally managed to phrase the question.

The man looked at him and then looked away before he responded. "I don't know the numbers, my boy, but I think the loss of life is pretty serious."

"My God, how could this happen?" Matthew whispered loudly enough for the man to hear him.

He looked at Matthew for a second and then looked away again. "I don't know, my lad. I just don't know," he said, and began to sob.

Matthew lay back down, looking up at the ceiling. He lifted up his hand, but it dropped weakly, sapped of strength. He was aware of movement. The man who had been sitting on the deck had stood up and was standing over him. Matthew started to speak, not sure if the man was even listening to him.

"I last saw him jump into the ocean, and I called out his name, but I don't think he even heard me… How can I go West without him?"

"You're delirious, boy. I'm going to get the doctor." The man hurried away, and Matthew couldn't form the words in his mind to stop him.

After eating and then sleeping a few hours, Andrew felt well enough to go out on deck. The *Carpathia* was circling the area of the sinking, looking for more survivors before returning to New York. Andrew saw several large icebergs and an ocean strewn with wreckage, deck chairs and oak paneling bobbing up from somewhere now far below. He pulled at the sleeve of the coat a passenger on the *Carpathia* had given him. The pants and shirt were also too long, but they felt better than his wet clothes, which were hanging to dry in the kitchen next to the ovens. Andrew finally turned away, unable to bear looking at the debris any more.

What if Matthew is out there, unable to call out? he asked himself.

He shook his head to clear his mind of such a morbid thought and began to walk away but stopped. William and Claire were sitting on a pair of deck chairs, and Claire was speaking to one of the officers he recognized from the *Titanic*. He stood back and listened to the end of the conversation, standing far enough away that they didn't see him.

"... Three pairs of good custom-made shoes... my teal silk Lucile dress with the bronze lace and buttons... all gone." She sobbed. William put an arm around her shoulder.

"Calm yourself, darling. Let me get you some coffee," William said. The officer stood over them, looking as if he wanted to be somewhere else, and then finally someone came along and whispered something to him. He walked away without speaking.

Andrew thought about stepping forward and saying something to them, but after what had happened between them on the *Titanic*, he couldn't bring himself to face them. Letting his parents know he was safe and finding Matthew were his first priorities.

Andrew waited in a line of other *Titanic* passengers who were sending off wireless messages, and when his turn came, an officer told him, "The wireless operator has his hands full at the moment, but he'll get your message off as quickly as he can."

"I understand. Send this message to my parents in Edinburgh whenever you can," Andrew said as he handed over the wireless form and then walked away.

Outside the dining room, Andrew saw someone familiar, standing in an ill-fitting coat and speaking with an officer. The officer nodded at Andrew and walked away.

"Colonel Gracie, I'm glad someone I know is here," Andrew said. He wanted to ask about Frank Millet and William Stead, but Mr. Gracie answered his unasked question.

"Mr. Millet and Mr. Stead didn't make it, I'm afraid."

Andrew understood, and after that they both remained at the rail, watching the faint wake of the ship's hull in the water.

Andrew let his mind wander; he wished he'd shared more with Matthew than furtive kisses and the one time they made love. He could have told Matthew a little more about Robert, how if it hadn't been for him, he would never have been on the *Titanic* to meet Matthew. Now he had to face the future. He would travel on alone to San Francisco, or somewhere that direction; perhaps he would like it there and settle down.

He thought about going to Texas and becoming a cowboy, just like Matthew had wanted.

That would be a fitting way to honor his memory, Andrew thought. He backed away from the rail and found a place to sit outside a portion of the dining room that had been turned into a makeshift hospital.

Andrew had only been sitting against the wall for a few minutes when an officer and a man in a navy-blue jacket, who had been watching him for a few minutes prior, approached him. He looked up.

"I know it might be too much to ask after what you've been through, but we need any able-bodied men to help us out in the hospital. Moving and helping the other survivors…" the officer said.

"I would be glad to help in any way I can," Andrew offered.

"Thank you, sir. Now, if you'll come with us," the officer in the blue jacket motioned for Andrew to follow him.

Matthew could feel his almost naked body sweating under the pile of wool blankets. Someone had laid an extra one over him and left only part of his face from the nose up exposed. His vision was still a little cloudy, but he could see three men walking past him.

Matthew blinked a few times, and his vision cleared enough to see the face of the third man, walking behind the other two—Andrew. He had been saved. But Andrew didn't look down to see Matthew lying covered up on the floor.

Where is he going? Why didn't he see me?

Chapter Twenty-One

Tuesday, April sixteen, 1912

Andrew sat on the floor to rest, a bowl of porridge cradled in his hands. It wasn't the dinner he had brought Matthew on that last night, but he was so hungry he ate two bowls and drank as many cups of coffee before he returned to work helping his fellow survivors. He talked to them about their experiences and consoled the women who had lost their husbands. He helped a little girl who was separated from her family and finally located her mother in the lounge. The woman thanked him in French, and he smiled and walked away.

In the dining room, Andrew poured coffee for a group of passengers, and he thought about the day he had taken over the duties of a steward in the third-class smoking room. He was so distracted that he almost spilled the coffee on his hand, but he pulled back just in time.

"The *Carpathia* is returning to New York, even though the *Titanic*'s sister ship *Olympic* has offered to take on the survivors…" Andrew overheard an officer telling someone, and he heard the person gasp and respond.

"The two ships were nearly identical. It would be like seeing a ghost. No, staying right here on the *Carpathia* would be a better option... Is it true that the White Star chairman Bruce Ismay is locked up in the doctor's cabin?"

"It's true, but I don't know much more than that..."

The two men walked out of the room before Andrew could hear any more. He closed his eyes and tried to picture Matthew, but he could only glimpse the last time he saw him, just before they'd jumped. He opened his eyes once again and sighed.

Matthew sat up and looked into the face of a man who was staring down at him, his hand pressed to Matthew's forehead.

"Well, it's a good sign you're coming around at last."

"How long have I been lying here? What day is it?"

"I'll answer both questions. It's April sixteenth, and you've been

drifting in and out on us since yesterday."

"I see... What ship is this?"

"You're on the Cunard liner *Carpathia*. We were on our way to the Mediterranean when we got the *Titanic*'s distress call. Relax, we're returning to New York," the doctor said.

Matthew threw aside one of the blankets, but the doctor gently pressed him back down.

"I would rest a few more hours before you get up, my boy, and I would recommend having someone bringing you some clothes first," the doctor said, then walked on to someone sitting in a chair nearby.

A few hours later, Matthew moved his legs over the side of the mattress and sat up. Dizzy, he put his head in his hands until it passed. He pushed himself to his feet and stood. Wrapping one of the blankets tightly around his body, he took a few unsteady steps toward a door. He met the doctor coming back in.

"See, Doctor, I'm just fine," Matthew said, bouncing on his heels and trying to convince him.

The man shook his head. "If you insist, but I wouldn't overdo it right away. I'll get you some clothes and see about getting you something to eat."

"Thanks," Matthew said.

In the dining room, Andrew was helping pour mugs of tea when someone called out to him.

"You there, could you bring some soup to a young man in the infirmary? He's dressed in a gray tweed suit and pants."

Andrew recognized the doctor, because he had spoken to him earlier. He nodded. "Sure, right away."

He found a tray and ladled some beef broth into a bowl, then carried it in. He saw the man sitting in a chair with his back to him when he entered. Andrew paused. There was something familiar about the back of the young man's head. He squeezed his eyes shut and reopened them, then walked up slowly.

"Matthew?" Andrew's voice barely came out, but the young man turned around.

The tray fell out of Andrew's hands and hit the floor with a crash. A second later, Matthew was in his arms.

"Andrew, I can't believe it's you."

"I thought I lost you," Andrew said. He looked Matthew up and down. Matthew's pants and the jacket were too small, and Andrew laughed between his tears of joy. "You look funny. They could have at least found clothes from someone your size."

"These are my clothes—I'm afraid they shrank a little. I could say the same thing about you. Did you get that off a giant?" Matthew said, taking Andrew in his arms once again. He was reluctant to let go, but he did at last. They looked down at the overturned bowl at their feet.

"I'm sorry I spilled your soup. Let me clean it up, and I'll get you something else." Andrew stooped and used a towel he had on the tray to clean the mess he'd made. He glanced up to see Matthew staring at him with a look of amusement on his face. "What? You've never seen me doing this before? I've been busy the past several hours helping out the crew of the *Carpathia*, doing whatever I can for our fellow survivors... There's probably just over seven hundred of us, I'm afraid," Andrew said.

Matthew bowed his head; he recalled someone saying the loss of life was serious, but he hadn't been told the numbers, or any other details.

"I've been asleep since yesterday. I haven't heard too many details yet," Matthew said quietly.

"I heard that Bruce Ismay is in the doctor's cabin on tranquilizers, telling people he has no right to be alive... Women and children are..." Andrew trailed off.

Matthew, who had been looking down at the floor, listening, raised his head. "Yet, you and I survived... I feel like I don't deserve to be..."

"We shouldn't feel guilty to be alive. We didn't run a ship full speed into an iceberg in the dead of night or let it sail with only enough lifeboats for half the people on board. They'll hold a routine inquiry, and nothing will change," Andrew said with a hint of bitterness.

Matthew reached out and held his hand. They didn't want to let go, but someone in the room coughed. Feeling suddenly self-conscious, Matthew released Andrew's hand.

"Come on, let's get you some food, and then we can talk," Andrew said, leading the way to the dining room.

Andrew stood close to Matthew, looking out over the ocean that pushed away in endless waves from the *Carpathia's* side. The sea was becoming rough, and the ship was bucking in the waves, causing spray to hit their faces. They didn't speak for a while; they stood together, trying to keep warm.

Finally, Matthew leaned closer to Andrew. "What happens to us now? You and me?"

"We continue on to New York, and then I'm going with you to your cowpoke ranch in Texas. Everything that's happened has only made me realize that life is too short and valuable to throw away," Andrew said.

He felt Matthew touch his hand lightly, and his fingers lingered there. "Have we changed, Andrew?" Matthew whispered.

"Maybe. I know I can never look at the world in the exact same way again. We only have the moment we're living in. Nothing is secure. I keep thinking that my mother was nervous about me going on that ship..." Andrew said, pointing out over the waves.

"You know, when I was locked up in that cabin, I was afraid of having to go back and face Lord Carson, but I don't feel the least bit nervous about that any more. We survived the sinking of the *Titanic*. I think I can face anything, even Lord Carson."

"You're going back? What about going to Texas, your dream of becoming a cowboy like in the pictures?"

"If I don't go back and defend myself against whatever the charges are, I won't be comfortable living with myself."

"I'll go back with you, and then we're going to pay a visit to my family. They can either accept me or cut me off, but either way, I won't be married." Andrew admired the confidence in his own voice, and he took a deep breath.

"What about William and Claire?" Matthew said.

"They are on the *Carpathia*. I'm afraid they might be biding their time, but I'll have to face them down eventually."

"Can I do anything to help… talk to them?"

"No, I have to stand up to them on my own, no matter what they do or say."

"Then I'll be with you."

"Thank you. I appreciate that," Andrew said, staring out over the waves. He loved feeling the nearness of Matthew next to him, and he wanted to kiss him, but he couldn't. "I love you," Andrew finally said, releasing all the words he had felt.

Matthew moved even closer, and whispered back, "I love you too, and when I thought I lost you, I didn't know what I was going to do." He looked down over the side of the ship, then slowly up into Andrew's eyes.

Andrew smiled. "You don't know how happy it makes me to hear you say that."

"Well, look what we have here, Claire, darling. The two lovebirds," William said, spitting out the last word like a curse.

Andrew and Matthew both turned around at the same time.

They faced William and Claire, with only two feet of distance between them. No one spoke for a moment; then Matthew broke the silence.

"I don't know what hold you two have on Andrew, but it's over right now, do you hear?" Matthew said.

"You're only a steward, so this whole matter doesn't concern you," Claire said, jerking her chin at Matthew. William stood by her, nervously looking from his sister to Andrew and Matthew, then out to sea and back again.

"You're wrong. It involved me the minute I met Andrew."

"What an admirable sentiment," William finally said.

"Claire, I don't want to marry you, not to please my father or for any other reason. Now, I'll pay your fare back home, and I'll pay whatever you want. I would take it if I were you. I can't marry a woman who is already married," Andrew said, indicating William.

"I see he told you." She turned on William. "You damned fool, you should have finished them both off when I told you to."

"I tried to, dear, but something always got in the way," William stammered. He turned to Andrew. "I should have left you in the water to freeze to death or shot you sooner, but…"

"Excuses. I should have done the job myself," Claire said.

"Don't do anything you're going to regret, Claire," Andrew warned. He looked around for a way out, but the ocean on one side and a bulkhead on the other surrounded them. He and Matthew were trapped.

"I won't regret it, and nobody will be any the wiser if you go missing. You're both going to be two more victims of the *Titanic*."

"You're nothing better than a cheating, lying bitch," Matthew said, taking a step toward the pair, but Andrew put a hand on his sleeve and stopped him.

"Such colorful language, but enough of this. Let's move to a more discreet place," Claire said.

"You're both going to be sorry," Andrew said.

Claire and William laughed, and Claire reached into her pocket and pulled out a small silver pistol.

"One of the things I saved from the ship. I knew it would come in handy someday."

"Can you stop talking, dearest, and get this over with?"

"All in good time, William."

"Bitch!" Andrew spat. He didn't normally swear at or in front of women, but now it felt appropriate.

William shoved him hard so he lost his footing and fell *face down* on the deck. Matthew helped Andrew to his feet and made sure he was all right.

"I'm fine, just a scrape." Andrew showed him a rope burn on his hand from falling against a coil of rope.

"Come on, you two, let's get moving. Over there, behind that deckhouse where they can't see us from the bridge," Claire said, urging them forward.

The *Carpathia* was rising and falling on the waves, and it was difficult for William and Claire to stand, but Andrew and Matthew were able to balance themselves against the pitch of the bow.

"It looks like we're as far forward as we can go, dear. What do we do now?" William said.

Claire turned up the collar on her coat with one hand and balanced by hanging on to William with the other.

"It looks like it's the end of the journey for the two of you. It'll be a shame when I send a wire to your parents, telling them that you didn't survive, after all… A mix-up, you understand." Claire smirked.

Andrew studied her face for a minute or two, looking for a way out. The sea was getting rougher. The waves were just enough to break over the bow, and now the deck at their feet was becoming slick.

Andrew stood with one foot on the rail and one on the deck. "Claire, let Matthew go, and I'll do whatever you want."

"You will? Will you agree to a sham marriage with me and give him up?" She pointed her pistol in Matthew's direction.

Andrew looked into Matthew's eyes. All he could think was *I love you, Matthew, but if this will keep us alive…*

"So do I, mate, you know I do," Matthew said out loud, reading his thoughts.

Less than a foot away, William and Claire were growing impatient, and at last Claire stamped her foot on the deck.

"Enough of the stalling. Let's say we accept your deal. What's to say you won't try to find each other later?" Claire scowled.

She took a step toward Andrew and Matthew, now pushed against the rail with nowhere to run. The bow plunged into another wave.

William nudged her. "Hurry up with this. I'm starting to turn green here," he snapped.

Andrew couldn't resist laughing. "Don't we get any last words?" he asked, hoping to buy a fraction of time.

"This isn't a Shakespeare drama, Mr. Elliot, but if you insist," Claire said.

Andrew was prepared to say something, but William suddenly shoved past Claire, rushed to the rail, hung over it, and was sick. Claire swore loudly. The distraction was enough for Andrew to grab the pistol out of Claire's hand.

He held the gun on them while Matthew moved around the deckhouse to attract the attention of a man who was passing by his head bowed down. When the man heard Matthew calling, he looked up, and Matthew recognized the face staring out from under the cap. Matthew was never so happy to see someone, aside from Andrew, in his life.

"Tom, thank God!"

"Good to see you, mate. What's going on here?"

"We have an appointment to see the captain with these two. I know he has his hands full, but when he hears what I have to say, then I think he'll find the time," Andrew said, motioning Claire and William to step away from the rail. "Come, you two, let's go and visit the bridge." Andrew nodded for the couple to move in front, while Matthew and Tom followed on either side in case they should run.

After Andrew's discussion with the captain, Claire and William were taken away under arrest and locked up in the master-at-arms' quarters.

Andrew remained on the bridge with Captain Rostron to write out a statement for the police in New York, and in between the words, he looked up and gazed at Matthew, who was outside on deck talking with his friend, Tom.

When Andrew finished writing, he went outside to join the two men at the rail.

"If I hadn't been assigned to a lifeboat after bringing a group of third-class passengers on deck, I wouldn't be here. So many of our mates…" Tom said. Matthew looked away out over the ocean. All three were silent, lost in their own thoughts.

Tom finally broke the silence. "What are your plans when we reach New York on Thursday?" he asked.

"We'll stay in New York for a few days, and then we'll return to England. If there's an inquiry, maybe we'll give a statement," Andrew said, hoping that he was speaking for Matthew. Matthew nodded, and he smiled.

"I'll give you my address in Southampton so you can write me. I wish you both good fortune," Tom said. He took a piece of paper from his pocket, wrote on it, and handed it to Matthew. They all shook hands, and then Tom walked away.

Andrew and Matthew sat on a couple of deck chairs, looking out over the rolling sea. Matthew smoothed the crease in his pants. He turned to look into Andrew's eyes.

"You know, I've been thinking, Andrew. I was a member of the *Titanic*'s crew, but everyone thinks I'm a passenger, especially when they took your coat from me when I was brought on board. I never got a chance to correct them."

"At least give them your real name. There can't be two Andrew Elliot's who survived the sinking." Andrew laughed.

"Will you come with me to straighten out the confusion?"

"Of course, I will." Andrew smiled.

Chapter Twenty-Two

Thursday, April eighteen, 1912

Andrew stood patiently beside Matthew in the pouring rain on the deck of the *Carpathia* as the tugboats slowly guided the ship into the Cunard Line dock. The shoreline growing ever closer was crowded with people who had braved the storm to greet the seven hundred and five passengers and crew of the two thousand two hundred who had set sail on the *Titanic* just over a week earlier.

"I'll be happy to set foot on land again, I won't deny it," Matthew said.

"It won't be too much longer now." Andrew shielded his eyes from the flash of newspaper cameras on the dock. He moved closer and put his arm through Matthew's.

They started at the grinding sound of the *Carpathia* coming at last alongside the dock as men on shore rushed about, grabbing heavy ropes to secure them. Andrew could now make out faces looking up at them and squinting in the drizzle to see if they could spot friends or family along the rail.

A door clanged open on the side of the ship, and the gangplank was moved into place. Andrew watched from their vantage point between two lifeboats. Some Cunard

Line crewmen stepped off the ship and conversed with someone on the dock, but he was too far to hear what was being spoken. Then a woman stepped down the gangplank, and a man approached her and led her through the crowd. Others soon followed as the disembarkation began in earnest, one by one stepping ashore, surrounded by relatives and reporters.

Andrew and Matthew were among the last *Titanic* passengers and crew to leave the ship and set foot on land. Their clothes were damp from the rain, and they were happy for the shelter of the terminal. Men from the newspapers ran up to them, trying to press money into their hands.

"Are you both from the *Titanic*? Give us your story... Anything you can tell us," they shouted, but Andrew and Matthew moved along, ignoring them.

They went into a corner of the shipping terminal to dry off, and they were still there when two policemen came down the gangplank with William and Claire in handcuffs. They passed about ten feet from Andrew and Matthew, and the last Andrew saw of them was between the heads of the crowd. Then Andrew turned away.

"I saw what I wanted to see. You know, it was William who pulled me into that lifeboat. I'm grateful that he did, but I guess they'll both pay for their dishonesty and attempted murder. Come on, let's go, Matthew," Andrew said with a faint smile.

Matthew took his hand and held it for a brief second. They both turned and took a last look at the

Carpathia before they walked outside the pier and into a waiting taxi.

Matthew opened his eyes and stared into the darkness of the suite at the Waldorf-Astoria. This was the first time in weeks he had slept so soundly in any type of bed, but he was wide awake now. He got out of bed, walked over to the window, and moved aside the damask curtains.

Even at this late hour, New York City was alive with motorcars and horse-drawn carriages passing by on the street below. There were lighted windows in the skyscrapers—the first buildings over ten stories Matthew had ever seen. He turned from the window, and in the faint light from the half-open door of the drawing room, he could see Andrew's sleeping form on the bed next to where he had lain. Andrew was muttering something in his sleep. Slowly Matthew returned and sat on the edge of his side of the bed. He studied the lines of Andrew's face in the dim light.

Andrew looked even younger than his twenty-three years. His face was freshly clean-shaven, and his red hair tousled by their lovemaking and the pillow under his head. His strong, muscular arms lay exposed on top of the down comforter. Matthew couldn't help but gaze on him and smile, and he wondered if Andrew had looked the same way while they were napping together on the *Titanic*'s last night. Matthew leaned over and kissed Andrew on the forehead, and he was startled when Andrew spoke.

"Hello. Having trouble sleeping?" Andrew's voice still sounded heavy from sleep. He opened his eyes and rolled to his side, then lifted himself up on an elbow to look at Matthew.

Matthew smiled at him. "Part of me couldn't sleep, but part of me was curious to see New York at night."

"What do you think of New York at night?"

"It looks too big and too noisy even at night. I think I'll prefer Texas," Matthew said, suddenly remembering that in two days, after some rest, they were going to return to England to face the detectives at Scotland Yard.

"It'll all work out with the Yard, you know? Perhaps Lord Carson has already forgotten; he'll be reading all about the *Titanic* in the papers for a while."

"I hope you're right, Andrew, but that might not make him forget about me," Matthew whispered as he leaned down toward Andrew, who pulled him close.

"Have I told you how handsome you are?" Andrew held him tight.

"Several dozen times. Are you trying to make me forget facing Scotland Yard?"

"Is it working?" Andrew asked with a slight smile.

Matthew nodded and lay back down with Andrew once again.

When Andrew opened his eyes, sunlight was filtering in through the parted curtains. He sat up in bed, and it was his turn to look at the young man who slept on his back next to him. Matthew's brown hair was falling over his eyes, and a beard the color of his hair was starting on his chin. Andrew reached over and ran his fingers down Matthew's arms.

Matthew opened his eyes, squinting at the bright sunlight; he covered his eyes with one hand. "Good morning, Andrew." He lifted his head for a kiss, which was interrupted by a knock on the door.

Andrew got out of bed and threw on a robe to answer the door. A bellboy handed him a message, but Andrew waited until he was back with Matthew to open it. He read it, and then looked at Matthew over the folded paper.

"It's a reminder for us to appear in the ballroom to speak to Senator Alden Smith at the inquiry into the *Titanic* sinking," Andrew said.

After a leisurely breakfast and a stroll, Andrew led Matthew back to the hotel for the inquiry hearing.

Andrew and Matthew sat at the back of the ballroom of the Waldorf-Astoria, listening to Senator Smith's opening statements about the sinking. Andrew looked around the room and recognized the White Star chairman, Bruce Ismay, and Colonel Gracie, who were seated across the room.

Matthew elbowed him lightly and pointed out the wireless officer who had stood on the overturned lifeboat with him that night, as well as one or two of the officers he knew because Tom had once identified them.

It was a long meeting, with questions and testimony about lifeboat capacity, time and location of events, and the number of iceberg warnings the *Titanic* had received that Sunday. Andrew was shocked to find out there had been a ship, the *Californian*, some ten to twenty miles away from the sinking. The crew of the *Californian* had seen the rockets and lights, but the captain hadn't been notified of these things, nor had the wireless operator gotten out of bed.

"How many more lives could have been saved?" Andrew whispered to Matthew as they listened.

Andrew and Matthew were later both sworn in and gave their statements before the break.

The next few days were busy. Andrew and Matthew returned to the ballroom to listen to further testimony from survivors, and they were summoned to the police station to talk to a detective assigned to William and Claire's case.

Andrew learned William and Claire were to be returned to England to face a number of charges, only some of which were related to their attempts on Andrew. It seemed they were suspects in a number of thefts and fraud schemes in New York, London, and Paris, and theft in Berlin and Cairo.

The rest of the time, Andrew and Matthew were free to buy new clothes and see the famous sights of New York City. In the evenings, they returned to the hotel and fell asleep in each other's arms.

Monday, April twenty-two, 1912

Less than a week after rejoicing at being back on land, Andrew and Matthew boarded another ship for the return voyage to England. Andrew watched from the upper deck as the ropes securing the small ocean liner to shore were hauled in and tugboats guided her passage down the Hudson River. When New York was finally far behind, and the ocean stretched out in front of them, Andrew led Matthew away from the rail and to their cabin. He shut the door behind them and slid the lock into place.

He loosened his tie and dropped it on the floor, then reached up and pulled off Matthew's tie and tossed it next to his. Collar buttons and shirt studs clinked into a bowl on the dressing table, along with celluloid collars. Pants and shirts were thrown on top of shoes and socks on the floor beside the bed. Andrew took Matthew by the hand and pulled him down onto the bed.

They shared a breathless, passionate kiss. Matthew ran his hands down Andrew's face to his neck and down his biceps to his waist. Andrew followed his example, exploring Matthew, before lying back on the bed and pulling Matthew on top of him.

Matthew kissed Andrew deeply, then trailed his kisses to Andrew's neck and chest, and down to his length, which Matthew then took into his mouth. Andrew closed his eyes and moaned at the warmth that surrounded him. He could feel Matthew's hair between his fingers and guided his head in a bobbing motion until Matthew came up for air. Then it was Andrew's turn to take him in his mouth. Andrew moved his way back up to Matthew's lips for another kiss. He kept his fingers on Matthew, using his hand to bring him to release. Andrew followed him a few moments later.

Andrew and Matthew lay holding each other, with their legs entwined, listening to their own breathing, the beating of their hearts, and the rumbling of the ship's engines down below.

"I love you, Matthew," Andrew whispered into Matthew's ear. Matthew shifted around slightly so he could turn his head to face Andrew and smile. Andrew pulled him forward for a kiss.

They lay looking into each other's eyes until they slowly fell asleep in each other's arms.

May six, 1912 Scotland Yard

Matthew paced the waiting room until Andrew looked up at him and caught ahold of his sleeve.

"Will you relax? Everything will be fine. The detective didn't look too gruff when we walked in, and the policeman with the moustache like a walrus probably looks at everyone with the same unflinching expression," Andrew said.

He was trying to make Matthew smile, and it almost worked. However, a man being led out in cuffs, pushed along by the police, made Matthew feel more anxious for what might happen.

Andrew finally got up and pressed him down into the bench. "I'll be right with you the whole time, remember that."

"Matthew Ahearn!" a man with a big moustache called in a deep voice.

Matthew took a step toward the man in the doorway, and Andrew followed.

"I'm going with him," Andrew informed the policeman.

"Suit yourself, sir, but I warn you to remain silent."

"Like we're in church," Andrew said. The man led Matthew and Andrew through a maze of hallways until they came to an open door. In the room, a man was seated at a desk looking at a stack of papers. Matthew knocked and stepped inside. His heart was pounding so loudly he could barely hear Andrew whispering encouragement or the sound of the papers being shuffled.

The man on the other side of the desk at last set his work aside and looked up at them. "Matthew Ahearn?"

"Yes, sir." Matthew's voice was so hoarse he could barely speak. The detective at the desk pushed back his chair.

"I'm sorry for the inconvenience, but the case against you has been dropped," he said.

"What did you say, sir?"

"The case has been dropped. Lord Carson doesn't want any trouble, so he dropped the case against you.

He asked me to give you this." The detective opened a drawer and took out a white envelope. He slid it across the desk to Matthew. "Good day, sir," the detective said, resuming his seat and going back to his work.

After they left the building, Matthew had to sit on a bench outside before he could do anything else.

"He dropped the case," Matthew repeated, slowly fingering the envelope's edges.

"See, I told you everything would work out just fine. I think Lord Carson must have realized you were innocent and let the case go. I'm so happy for you, Matthew," Andrew said, putting an arm around Matthew's shoulders.

Matthew looked from the object in his hands to Andrew's eyes. "Thank you for standing by me, Andrew. I love you."

"Love you too, mate. Now see what that letter says," Andrew said.

Matthew's fingers trembled as he tore open the seal and removed the contents. He read the note to Andrew.

Matthew, I'll wager you're surprised to receive a letter from me, but I felt compelled to write. I read about your experience aboard the ill-fated Titanic in the Times. A sad tragedy for everyone involved.

The police may or may not have informed you that the real thief who attacked me was a regular resident of that hotel and has been apprehended. He confessed to several other crimes in the same area.

Sorry to have caused you trouble. I've had all the charges against you dropped. Good luck in the future.

Lord Carson

"That's all," Matthew said, folding the piece of paper and slipping it into his pocket.

"That's a reason to celebrate, isn't it?" Andrew said.

Matthew looked down at the sidewalk and then into Andrew's face. He was genuinely happy because it meant he was truly free. He had wanted to confront Lord Carson and ask why the man had accused him and had him hunted down. But he let the simmering anger fade; he'd at least gotten an apology, even if it was not in person.

Matthew felt the warmth of Andrew's body next to his calm him. "At least it's over, Andrew. Let's go now."

Highlands of Scotland May, 1912

It took an hour and a half to drive from Inverness to Lochindorb and the country manor house owned by the Elliot family. When Matthew got out of the car, happy to stretch his legs at last, he looked up at the stone building and far across the lake at the ruins of Lochindorb Castle in the distance, accessible only by boat.

"So, it's not exactly a castle, but we take the name from the ruins over there." Andrew pointed. They followed the footman, Douglas, who accompanied them into the house.

"I'll start a fire, sir. It'll take the chill away." The servant's voice echoed in the drafty great hall hung with paintings and weapons.

When he was gone, Andrew pulled a flask of whisky from his pocket and, smiling, handed it to Matthew. "This will take any cold away too," Andrew said mischievously.

Matthew took a fast swig, choking and almost spitting the contents at Andrew and the painting of the ancestor behind him. Andrew raced to pat him on the back. Douglas was back by then to announce the fire was going in the library and he would bring the luggage up to their separate rooms.

Andrew led Matthew to the library, then excused himself and stepped back into the hallway. Finding Douglas returning with their bags, Andrew asked, "What happened to Mr. Craig and his son? I haven't seen them anywhere."

"Well, Mr. Craig accepted a position at another estate in the south, as gamekeeper, I believe, and his son, Robert, I think his name was, is a captain in the Army in India. He married recently. Mrs. Morgan, the housekeeper, got a letter from him. I understand your father has employed a new grounds and gamekeeper."

"I'm happy for him," Andrew said. "Thank you."

Andrew returned to the library and leaned against the door for a moment. *So, Robert is in India and married,* he mused, hoping that Robert was as happy as he was with Matthew.

He opened the door and joined Matthew on the sofa in front of the flames crackling in the fireplace.

Andrew kissed Matthew, and they held each other while they stared out the tall windows overlooking a small cliff with a view of the castle ruins. After the room had warmed comfortably, Andrew rose and led

Matthew to the windows to get a better view.

"It's nice here, Andrew. Have you ever been out to the ruins?" Matthew asked.

"If you don't mind rowing, we can go over there tomorrow. It's more a wildlife sanctuary now, so lots of people go there to hunt or fish from the shore. This time of year, it will be pretty quiet," he said with a slight smile toward Matthew.

The next day, after rowing out to explore the ruins of the castle, they wandered among the heather that grew there and fished along the banks of the loch. They returned to the house in early afternoon.

The footman laid out lunch for them in front of the fire, and Andrew saw two letters next to his plate. He recognized his father's writing on one, and he slowly tore it open, dreading whatever his father might have to say.

Andrew,

After much soul-searching, I have reached a decision. While I don't agree with your choices, I think that going to Texas, as you mentioned, would be the best thing for you. I have spoken with Mr. Hamilton, our solicitor, and he is preparing to release to you the share of the inheritance that belongs to you. I'm sure you'll find it more than adequate to provide for your needs if you invest wisely, but I don't need to tell you that.

Your mother and I will be coming to the estate in three weeks, and we shall discuss this and other matters when we arrive.

Your mother sends her love. Your affectionate father

He tore open the second letter, and read through it silently, and he had to stop his fingers from trembling with excitement by the end.

Andrew Elliot.

I have done the research you requested in your letter. I was able to locate for you a small ranch in Texas, somewhere outside a place called Dallas. (Wherever that is.) There's only twenty-five acres, a small ranch house, and a dozen head of cattle already on the property. Let me know if you are interested.

J. Hamilton, Solicitor

Andrew let out a yelp, and Matthew asked, "Is everything all right, mate?"

"Everything is fine, Matthew. My parents are coming to see us in a few weeks," Andrew said. He decided to keep the possible purchase of the ranch a secret until they were back in London in October.

Later that day, after they'd explored more of the countryside on horseback, they returned to the house in the late afternoon, just as the rain began to fall in torrents again.

They were both soaking wet and laughing as they ran through the great hall and fell down on the thick carpet in front of the library fireplace. There was a fire, lit by Douglas who had then withdrawn to the servant's quarters. Andrew and Matthew lay together on the floor, listening to the crackle of the logs and the pounding of the rain on the windows. Andrew could still see his father's letter folded on the library table. Matthew reached out and touched Andrew's cheek, flushed from the fire.

"I wish I knew what was on your mind. You look like you have some important news to share, and you're keeping it from me, mate," Matthew said softly, sliding closer to Andrew.

Andrew smiled. "I guess I can't keep it from you until October…"

"Keep what? What are you hiding from me?" Matthew asked, playfully punching Andrew's arm.

"Okay, I might as well tell you. We're going to be the proud owners of a ranch in Texas."

"What? Am I hearing you right, mate?" Matthew asked, smiling nervously.

"You sure are. All I need to do is sign the papers. I can't wait to tell my parents when they come up here."

"I don't think I've ever been so happy in my life, Andrew. What about your father? He's not exactly happy with our relationship."

"He's not, but as long as he's extending the olive branch, it would be a wise move to take it. He could withdraw it."

Andrew and Matthew went upstairs after dinner, and they lay together in the giant bed in Andrew's room, listening to the wind howl and the rain beat against the windows. They chose not to bother with the pretense of the separate rooms.

"The fire is dying…" Andrew indicated the fireplace on one side of the room, where the embers cast shadows from the heavy furniture into the corners.

Matthew snuggled closer to Andrew under the covers.

"You're freezing, Matthew." Andrew kissed his lips.

Matthew smiled. "A ranch in Texas…"

"Texas," Andrew repeated happily. It didn't matter where they went, as long as Matthew was with him.

They made love with the shadows dancing over them, and then

they fell asleep in each other's arms, listening to the haunting moans coming from either the wind or phantoms around the house.

One Year Later The Texas Plains

Epilogue

In October of 1912, they had sailed back to America to begin their lives together as ranchers on the plains of Texas. The ranch was a work in progress—the plumbing was still outdoors, something that took getting used to, and there was no electricity yet.

"We don't need electricity to work the gramophone," Andrew said cheerfully as he put on a record and wound up the machine before leading Matthew through the steps of the turkey trot.

Matthew thought about their life together and he smiled.

"What are you smiling about?"

"I don't think you will believe it, but I've never been so happy in my life."

"I believe it, because I could say the same thing to you," Andrew said. "I've never been happier, Matthew. If I hadn't lost my cap that night aboard the *Titanic*, I would have never met you, and I probably would have—"

"Don't say that, Andrew. We're together right now, and that's what matters most," Matthew said. "I thought we agreed to not talk about it?" Matthew gently reminded Andrew that they had made a pact never to talk about that night. The only exception had been the interview they gave to the newspaper in Dallas when they first arrived.

"I know we did, but it's been on my mind lately."

"I'll never stop hearing those cries after the sinking," Matthew admitted, closing his eyes and shaking his head, trying to get rid of the memory.

Matthew never let Andrew know that he knew Andrew still had bad dreams about that night, once or twice reaching out for some imaginary object in his sleep. Matthew understood. He put his arm around Andrew and pulled him closer.

Andrew lifted his gaze to Matthew. "Sometimes when I close my eyes, I see the ship breaking in half. For a second, the sparks lit up a torn- open cabin, but then it was gone," Andrew said.

"I just missed being struck by one of the funnels when we fell. The wave was what pushed me closer to the capsized boat." It was the first time Matthew had spoken of what had happened in the water.

"Thank you for talking about it with me," Andrew said.

It was already dark as they walked to the window and pushed back the curtains. The Texas heat had cooled down, and a slight breeze swept over them. The sky was bright with stars, and Andrew let his mind wander back to another starry night.

"Will I ever be able to forget, or will April fiftewn be a part of me forever?" He thought he had spoken to himself, but Matthew put his arm around his waist and pulled him closer to kiss him.

"I always wonder that same thing, and I guess the answer is that night will always be a part of us, and we'll have to live with it. It shaped the men we are today."

"I hope that means we're good men who happen to love each other, because I love you, Matthew," Andrew said, feeling Matthew's hand searching for his and grabbing it tightly.

"I know I love you, Andrew, and you don't have to worry. I think we're doing pretty well."

Later that night they took their blankets outside and made love under the stars. Afterward, they lay together looking up into the sky and then fell asleep dreaming about the future.

THE END